Sweet Forever

Jillian Hart

Copyright © 2014 by Jill Strickler
All rights reserved.
http://jillianhart.net

Cover Design by The Killion Group
http://hotdamndesigns.com

E-book Formatted by Jessica Lewis, Authors' Life Saver
http://authorslifesaver.com

This is a work of fiction. Names, characters, places, brands, media, and incidents are either the product of the author's imagination or are used fictitiously. The author acknowledges the trademarked status and trademark owners of various products referenced in this work of fiction, which have been used without permission. The publication/ use of these trademarks is not authorized, associated with, or sponsored by the trademark owners.

ISBN: 1499711220
ISBN-13: 978-1499711226

CHAPTER ONE

Bluebell, Montana Territory, January 1867

Snow fell from steel-gray clouds, swirling and dancing in mid-air. Penelope Shalvis hiked her book bag higher on her shoulder, drew her scarf a little higher over her throat and tilted her head back to gaze up at the sky. Snowflakes pummeled her face and caught in her eyelashes. What a sight. Even blinking against those white flakes, she couldn't get enough of the wonder of nature. Look at the way the snow waltzed, spiraling and dipping. Such beauty. It lifted a girl's spirits. It felt like anything was possible.

She heard the distant *clip-clop* of an approaching horse and snapped to attention, rubbing snow off her face. The last thing she wanted was to be caught staring into space like a simpleton--as her stepmother would say. Her stepmother back home in Boston didn't put a lot of value in stopping to appreciate nature.

"Penelope!" a familiar, friendly voice called out. "Is that you?"

"Rose!" Delighted to see her friend, she rushed over to the approaching horse and sleigh. "What are you doing out so early?"

"Emergency supply run." Rose McPhee explained, blond curls peeking out from beneath her wool hood. She pulled Wally, her giant buckskin gelding, to a stop. Bundled in her sleigh, she looked adorable. "Iris ran out of eggs for this morning's baking, so I'm racing over to the Meeks' farm so there will be no warfare between my sisters. It's way too early in the morning for that."

"Did someone miscount the eggs you had on hand?" Penelope asked, amused as always by the McPhee sisters. Life at McPhee Manor was never dull.

"Of course. Magnolia was sure we had enough in the cellar, but she was wrong. When Iris grabbed the basket that was supposed to be full, it was empty. Chaos ensued, so here I am, out and about in this cold." Rose shivered, pulling the buffalo robes she was wrapped in all the way to her chin. "You must be heading to the schoolhouse and look at you. You're frozen. You're completely white with snow."

"It isn't the first time." Penelope brushed at her snow-covered coat and gestured to a nearby house with a snowman standing in what used to be a front lawn. "If I went and stood in that yard, no one would notice. They might give me a carrot for a nose, but otherwise, I'd be just like all the other snowmen."

"A snow *woman*," Rose teased in her gentle way. "I can turn around and drop you off at the school. Come on and climb in."

"I appreciate that, but I'm used to walking." It was only a few blocks to the school where she worked, teaching the town's children. Far too short of a distance to bother with her own horse and sleigh. Far better to leave her dear Alice snug and warm in her stall in this kind of weather. She shrugged. "Besides, you're in a hurry. I don't want Iris to have to wait for those eggs."

"Yes, poor Iris." Rose winked. "It's hard being the oldest sister of the bunch of us. We're trouble."

"Trouble of the best kind," Penelope agreed, nearly knocked off her feet when the wind gusted. "I'd better get going. It's going to take a while for the schoolhouse to heat up in this bitter cold."

"Okay." Rose snapped the reins and her big horse, Wally, leaped to attention, dragging the sleigh forward. "Have a great day!"

"You, too!" Penelope sang out, but the wind gusted again, tangling her skirts as Rose zipped away in her cute sleigh. Alone again, Penelope trudged on, plowing through the deep, fresh snow.

Rose was in such a good mood these days, and it was wonderful to see her happy. Who wouldn't be with a devoted beau like Seth Daniels, the local livery man? It was a perfect match. There was a lot of that going around, Penelope thought with satisfaction as she bowed her head, blinking hard against the beat of snow against her face. She liked knowing true love was out there. It happened more often than she used to think.

The schoolhouse loomed up like a dark giant, the bell tower disappearing into the shroud of falling snow. Glad to be where she belonged, she unlocked the door, stomped the snow off her shoes and shook it from her coat. Teeth chattering, she rushed to light a lamp and then the pot-bellied stove in the center of the room. Her movements echoed around her--the rasp of the match, the flare of the flame, the clink of the stove's damper as she opened it wide. All pleasant sounds, sounds that had become a wonderful part of her new life.

When she'd accepted the teaching position many months back, sight unseen, she'd feared she might be teaching in a hut or a hovel or even an Indian teepee. She'd never been out West before and she'd had no notion what to expect. But after her heartbreak in Boston, she was ready for anything as long as it was a fresh start.

With the fire successfully started, she lit the lamp on her desk. Golden light fell across the polished surface and she grabbed a stick of chalk from her top drawer. She caught sight of the ruler tucked there, for discipline purposes the superintendent had told her, but so far she hadn't had to use it. As rambunctious as the Dunbar twins were, the boys hadn't been truly naughty. In fact, all her students were a pleasure to teach. Her chest ached with love for them. They were all special, each and every one.

Smiling, she opened her calendar journal, full of her day's schedule and lesson plans. She lifted the chalk to the top left-hand corner of the blackboard and wrote the day's date. *Wednesday, January 12.* She took a step back and stared at the white letters and numbers, stark against the black background. It took a moment before realization pummeled through her. She blinked, staring at the date. Her chest tightened. Her stomach cramped up. Sweat broke out on her brow.

How could she have forgotten? She gasped, unable to take her eyes away from the date. Today, January 12, should have been her wedding day. Sorrow dug in, sharp and painful, and refused to let go. Memories of her dreams and dearest plans mocked her, all gone, all broken. She put down the chalk, drawing in a careful breath, and covered her face with her hands. Why did she have to go and remember? It only brought a mountain-load of hurt and humiliation.

"Miss Shalvis?" A man's uncertain voice echoed in the room.

Startled, she jumped, whipped around to see the town's attorney standing in the inner doorway. Snow covered him from head to toe, even clinging to the frames of his spectacles. "Mr. Denby. Goodness, I didn't hear you come in."

"You seemed to be in another place. You must have a lot on your mind." He offered her a tight, self-conscious smile. He was handsome in his own way with a rectangle face, blue eyes the color of indigo and thick brown hair. He wasn't a stand-out kind of handsome--more like the comfortable kind. He'd never talked to her before, other than a few formal brief encounters at various town gatherings. He arched one dark brow at her. "We can come back later, if it's better for you."

"We?" That's when she saw the spindly, ragamuffin little girl standing two steps behind the man.

"Well, hello there." Penelope's heart simply melted. Look at that pixie face. What a precious dear. "My name is Miss Shalvis, and I'm the teacher here. Come on in and sit close to the fire. You must be so cold."

The girl nodded, saying nothing. Her eyes, the same blue as Nathaniel's, were sad. Very sad.

"This is Evie, my niece." Nathaniel's deep voice warmed as he turned to the child. "Go on, go get warm. I need to speak with the teacher."

A niece? Penelope considered that. The girl's clothes were clearly secondhand. Maybe even thirdhand. She had the look of a poorly-fed child. There was a weariness to her, as if she'd been neglected for a long time. Penelope headed over to talk privately with Nathaniel in the foyer, her heart aching.

"A man I didn't know showed up at my office late yesterday." He lowered his voice, so it wouldn't carry. "He said he was Evie's uncle, on my sister's husband's side, and left her with me. He didn't even ask, just threw her satchel on the floor, told her to stay and rode off."

"How difficult for her, and what a surprise for you." Penelope peeked around the doorway. Yes, the girl was standing before the stove, hands out, warming herself. She looked so small and helpless from behind, with that little straight, stark part in her hair, right down the center. Two brown braids, rather inexpertly plaited, hung down her back. Penelope gave a little sigh. "No preparation time for you, and for her to be dumped off like that."

"She hasn't said a word to me, not one, since she arrived." Nathaniel took off his Stetson and raked a hand through his hair. "I don't know the first thing about a kid, but I do know she needs to be in school."

"She'll be well taken care of here, don't you worry." Penelope read the caring in Nathaniel's eyes, shining in that deep, mesmerizing blue. Really an incredible shade of blue. "I'll set some time aside this morning to evaluate her reading skills, see what level she's at. If she can join the other classes, great. If not, I'll work with her individually until she catches up with her class. She's not the only student I'm working with like that, so don't worry."

"I can see she'll be in good hands." Nathaniel hesitated. "I packed her a lunch. It's in the pail on the shelf in the vestibule. Does she need anything? I didn't know about books and a slate."

"She'll need those. I'll send a list home with her. You can get everything she needs at the mercantile." Penelope reached out for him, her touch encouraging as it landed lightly on his sleeve. "I'll lend her what she needs for today. I keep spare books and slates on hand just for this kind of thing, so no need to worry."

"Great. That's nice of you."

She smiled gently up at him, opening her mouth to speak. In fact, she kept speaking but he couldn't hear a word of it. Not one word.

Was something wrong with his hearing? Nathaniel blinked, puzzled, trying to figure it out. In fact, he couldn't hear anything at all. The world went silent as Penelope kept talking, moving her lovely mouth, as soft and as pink as rose petals, gazing up at him with compassionate hazel eyes that made his heart beat harder and faster.

Uh oh, he thought. He'd felt like this before, not quite as strongly but he definitely recognized it. He was attracted to the schoolteacher.

"I'll get her settled." Her voice came to him now, as if from far away. "I'll sit her with a girl her age, I have one in mind. Sadie's sitting in a desk by herself because she tends to be trouble, but she's a friendly girl and very kind. That might help to bring Evie out of her shell."

"Sounds good. Is this Sadie Gray, the sheriff's girl?"

"Yes. I hope that's not a problem?" Penelope narrowed her gaze at him as if trying to judge his reaction. "I know she's a bit of a tomboy and there are plenty of folks who don't approve of that, but I think it's good for a girl to be a child while she can. Restrictions and behavioral expectations come soon enough."

"Right." He hadn't given the notion of a tomboy much thought.

Except that little Sadie Gray was notorious for wearing trousers after school and for playing sports with boys her own age.

Then again, if it brought Evie out of her shell, he didn't care if she wore chaps and a bowler hat. He glanced through the inner doorway into the classroom where his niece had sunk into a desk, facing the aisle and the stove. Her slumped little shoulders and bowed head gave her a dejected look. His chest twisted up with helplessness, not knowing what to do for her.

"Please do everything you can." He meant that with all his heart. He didn't know Evie. In fact, he'd never seen her before. He'd only received a few letters from his sister mentioning the girl before her tragic death from scarlet fever. He ached for the loss of his sister and for her daughter's plight. He'd loved his baby sister, so he was determined to do right by Evie. Whatever it took.

"It's plain to see you're having a hard time leaving her." The warmth and understanding in Penelope's voice mesmerized. Captivated. Made him look at her--*really* look.

She could be a princess with her beauty, an angel with her good heart. Her lustrous brown hair shone with highlights of red and gold in the lamplight, as if a master painter had rendered her from nothing but color and light. She had the type of face a man couldn't look away from--quietly beautiful, but that beauty was powerful, because it was gentle. He blinked, more than a little dazed, and unprepared to be so.

He was a man of law, a man of books. Logic and knowledge dictated his life. It was the code he lived by. But his heart rolled over, thumping hard, captivated.

Don't even think about it, he told himself. Every time he followed his heart, he wound up overlooked and passed over for a more exciting man. The smart thing to do was to tip his hat politely to the schoolteacher, turn around and mosey right out the door. Don't look back or hesitate. Just keep on going--and that's exactly what he'd do.

"Have a good day, Evie," he called out. "I'll be outside waiting for you when school's over."

The girl nodded once in acknowledgement, keeping her back to him. She looked isolated sitting there and it pulled at him. He remembered what it was like when his mother had died and his family fell apart. He knew what it was like to be a child with no parent to love you, no one who cared. Turning on his heels, he headed out the door and hurried on his way. It felt as if he'd left a part of himself behind.

* * *

Interesting man. Penelope searched through her bottom desk drawer, not exactly sure why Nathaniel Denby stayed on her mind. She scooped up the secondhand slate and plopped it on the desk top, searching for the slate pencil. It was here somewhere. She searched for it, but her thoughts returned to the love and concern she'd seen unmistakably in his dark blue eyes. Little Evie was lucky to have him. It was as simple as that.

She spotted the pencil, fished it out from behind a hefty volume of Shakespeare and climbed to her feet. A handful of students had arrived, but that was all, and here it was almost time for school to start. Parents must be worried about the storm, she decided. Not that she blamed them. The wind howled, driving a chill through the walls, and she shivered.

"Good morning, Miss Shalvis." Bea McPhee sauntered by looking lovely in a pretty pink wool dress. Matching ribbons adorned her twin blond braids. "I did all my homework, every last bit of it, and didn't have any trouble at all."

"Most excellent. I expected as much. You are doing beautifully with your studies." Penelope beamed with pride for the girl. As Bea headed down the aisle toward her seat, Penelope grabbed up the old books and the battered slate and carried it to Evie's desk.

"These will be yours for the day," she explained. "I don't know if these are the correct level books for you yet, but I guessed. After I set the morning lessons, I'll have you come up to my desk and we'll see what you know."

Evie blinked her wide, indigo-colored eyes and nodded once.

"Miss Shalvis?" Sadie Gray clomped to a stop next to her seat, staring at the new girl occupying the other side of the double desk. "Do I really get a seatmate? You said that would never happen, not ever again. Not even when the world ends and all the stars fall from the sky."

"I did say that." Penelope bit the inside of her mouth to keep from smiling. "But today I've changed my mind. Don't disappoint me, young lady."

"I'll try not to." Sadie scrunched up her button face earnestly. "But you know how I am. I can't help it."

Penelope suspected as much. She bit the inside of her cheek a little harder. "Perhaps it would be wise to learn to button your lip when school is in session."

"But I'd need a button and a buttonhook for that." Sadie's eyes twinkled with good humor. The troublemaker was too charming for her own good.

And Penelope adored her for it. "Was that cheeky? It sounded a little cheeky."

"Maybe a little, but I'll be good. I promise." Sadie rolled her eyes. "Or at least I'll try really, really hard. When I remember to."

"I suppose that's a good start. Sadie, I'd like you to meet Evie." Penelope focused her attention on the withdrawn little girl, who stared hard at the slate on the desk in front of her. She looked uncomfortable with the attention. "Evie is new to town, so it would be very nice of you to make her feel comfortable here. You girls try not to get into too much trouble now."

"We won't," Sadie promised. "I swear it on my honor. Or, uh, I swear on my honor that I'll at least try."

You had to love that girl. Penelope bit her lip to keep from laughing out loud, turned on her heels and marched down the aisle. Most of the students were settling into their desks, although half the seats were empty. When she glanced at the clock on her desk, it was two minutes to eight. Nearly time for school to start.

She felt an arctic breeze gust through the doorway to the vestibule and headed toward it, wondering if the Dunbar boys had arrived and left the door open again. She wasn't at all surprised to find the twins covered with snow, wrestling off their wraps.

"Good morning, boys." She intended to remind them about the door, but they were half-frozen (they had a long walk to school every morning). "Be sure and warm up well at the stove before taking your seats."

"Yes, Miss Shalvis," Danny answered in his polite way, his black hair completely white with snow.

"We have to. Cuz if we don't, we might turn to solid ice." Devin lifted his arms like the abominable snowman and stomped toward his twin. "We'd be ice monsters."

"Miss Shalvis, he's lurching at me."

"That's because ice monsters lurch."

She caught hold of Devin before the wrestling could begin. With one hand she closed the outside door tightly and with the other she gave the boy a gentle but determined push in the direction of the classroom. "Go lurch to the stove and warm up. No horsing around in front of the stove, boys."

"Yes, Miss Shalvis." They said in unison, one giving the other an elbow in the ribs (and getting one in return) as they raced through the inner doorway.

"Walk!" She reminded them. She stepped over the mess of snow they'd left on the floor (she'd come back and sweep it up once she had lessons going). She intended to follow them into the room, but something caught her attention. A shadow in the shape of a man stood in the schoolyard, alone in the falling snow. She stared out the window, recognizing that fine wool coat and matching Stetson. Nathaniel Denby was still out there. He hadn't been able to walk away and leave his niece.

Her heart warmed against her will. See, there were good men in this world. It encouraged her, it gave her hope. After what she'd been through with Alexander, she'd been sure there wasn't a man in existence who had honor in him. But time spent here in Bluebell, Montana Territory had softened that opinion somewhat. There were good men in this world, and it was clear Nathaniel Denby was one of them.

She offered him a smile and a wave before waltzing away. She had students to teach and lessons to implement. The warmth and light met her as she closed the vestibule's inner door to trap the heat inside the classroom. Cheerfully, she called her students to order, ready to start another wonderful, albeit wintry day.

CHAPTER TWO

The storm was getting worse and it worried her. Penelope chewed her bottom lip, listening to the wind beating against the north side of the schoolhouse. The high, sweet voice of Sadie's younger sister, Sally, faltered.

"Is it a *K?*" The little girl asked, holding up her hands helplessly.

"No." Penelope turned her full attention to the three students standing shoulder to shoulder in front of her. Her seven-year-olds, and her youngest students. She ached, seeing how hard Sally was struggling.

"Think of the word," she advised, eager to help. "Can you see it in your head?"

"Are you sure we hafta learn to spell?" Sally's button face scrunched up adorably.

"I'm absolutely certain." Penelope closed her book and leaned forward in her chair. "Spelling is hard, but you can do this. I know you can. Here's a hint. Maybe it's not just one letter but two you have to think of. What makes a *ch* sound?"

"Ooh, I know." Hailie fidgeted next to Sally, eager to help out her friend. "Can I say it, Miss Shalvis?"

She smiled at adorable Hailie. "That's wonderful, but first let's let Sally think a little more. I know she can do it." She had absolute faith in the sweet girl. "Listen to the word. Chicken."

Sally puckered up one side of her face, thinking hard, but she was fated not to finish her spelling attempt. The wind hit the side of the schoolhouse so hard, the entire building shook. The windows rattled in their panes. The stove clanked and smoke coughed out the door. It was as if twilight had fallen. Worry gripped her.

The youngest girl, standing on the other side of Hailie, started to cry.

"I'm s-scared of st-torms," Ilsa stuttered, tears spilling down her cheeks.

"It's all right, Ilsa. You're perfectly fine. I'll take care of you." Penelope had been just like that as a little girl, afraid of the winter storms that used to pound Massachusetts, so it was easy to empathize. She pulled out a clean, folded handkerchief from her dress pocket and dabbed at Ilsa's face. "Do you want to stay up here with me and hold my hand, or do you want to go back to your desk?"

"I'll st-stay with y-you." Ilsa gripped Penelope's hand hard, fighting down sobs.

"It looks as though you have a reprieve, Sally." Penelope couldn't help winking at the little imp who gave a secret smile of relief. "Maybe you will use your time this afternoon to actually study your spelling words?"

"Okay." Sally didn't even look guilty--or particularly determined to study. She gladly took off with Hailie, leaning together and whispering on their way back to their shared desk.

Penelope straightened her shoulders. Well, it looked as if she would need to have another little talk with the sheriff. Frowning, she glanced at her clock. Quarter to noon. Far too early to think about dismissing school and yet she was responsible for the children's safety. What if the storm grew worse? Well, that made the decision for her. She launched to her feet.

"Boys and girls, school will be dismissed early." She paused while cheers rose up, echoing in the pleasant room. "For those of you who have a long walk home and wish to eat your lunch quickly before you go, I'll stay and keep the fire going for you. For those of you who live in town, you may leave now."

Instantly, chaos erupted. The boys jumped out of their seats, calling out to one another, their joy contagious. They pounded toward the vestibule door and flung it open with a bang, stomping as they went.

"Miss Shalvis?" Ilsa nudged in closer. "I live in town but I-I don't want to go out there."

"How about if I walk you home?" She offered, reaching for the dust cloth to wipe down the blackboard from the morning's lessons. "Will that make you feel better?"

"Yes, ma'am." Ilsa nodded sweetly, her red ringlet curls bouncing in rhythm.

Simply adorable. Penelope smiled. "Then you go tell your big sister to wait for me. We have to stay here until all the other children are ready to go home."

"Okay." Ilsa scurried off, leaving Penelope to finish cleaning her board. When she went to erase away the date, January 12, her hand hesitated. Pain brewed in her midsection as she remembered choosing her wedding dress in the fancy shop in Boston. Her sister's tinkling laughter came to her. How happy they'd all been on that day.

Alexander's betrayal still hurt. She forced it down, erasing the date on the board with great determination. If only she could wipe away her memories of him as easily.

"Don't hit me!" Danny Dunbar gave his twin a grin before giving him a shove across the floor.

Devin grinned back. "That wasn't a hit."

"It was too."

"It wasn't. This is a hit." He bunched up his fist, eager to demonstrate.

Penelope caught his arm just in time, the cutie. "Outside, you two troublemakers. Make sure you put your hat on, Danny. Devin, button up your coat all the way. Will you two be warm enough, or should I get my horse and sleigh and drive you home?"

"Nah, we'll be okay," Devin assured her, stopping in the doorway to give her a cheeky wink. "That storm ain't nuthin'."

She chuckled. Surely the storm would not be as fearsome as the Dunbar twins out there on the loose. She waved goodbye to the boys, checked on Ilsa who was snuggled up in front of the stove next to her sister, and then went to fetch her broom.

While she thoroughly swept the floor, the rest of the children finished eating, warmed up really well at the stove and left. She looked up to find Evie, Nathaniel's niece, still at her desk, hunched over her empty lunch pail. Was something wrong? Why was the girl still here? She had a short walk to Nathaniel's office. Concern rushed through her, and she put the broom away in the closet.

"Evie." She gentled her voice and handed the child her worn and ragged coat. "Why don't you get bundled up? You should be getting home."

Evie took her winter wraps without a word and nodded miserably.

Penelope's heart tugged so hard, it cracked a little. "Do you know the way home?"

Evie stared hard at her shoe, the one with a hole in the toe, and shook her head ever so slightly.

Okay, her heart was seriously going to break over this child. Penelope swallowed hard to keep her emotions out of her voice. "Well, that's actually a silver lining. This way I get the chance to walk you home. I don't know about you, but I like walking when I have good company."

Evie lifted one shoulder in a shrug, stood up and slipped one arm into her coat sleeve.

"Girls, we're almost ready to go. We're lucky the storm isn't too bad yet." She smiled at Ilsa and big sister Ida before opening the stove's door and banking the ashes. "We'll get you home to your ma, Ilsa. That's a promise."

Ilsa slipped off the seat beside her sister and landed with a thud. Her little mouth was pinched up tight with worry, but she gave a little sigh. Unable to resist, Penelope knelt to help Ilsa with her coat buttons.

As soon as the children were bundled up well, she ushered them outside. She locked the door, pocketed the key and took Ilsa and Evie by the hands. The instant she sank into the drifted snow, she knew she'd done right canceling school. They were in near white-out conditions. Snow might be magical, but not when it was blowing sideways, nearly blinding her. She felt confused, even on the street she knew by heart. They made it to the intersection, turned left and walked the sisters up to their doorstep.

"Miss Shalvis!" Rhoda Collins whipped open the door, her gaze arrowing straight to her little girls. "I was worried. I was about to put on my coat and come get them."

"We beat you to it." Penelope loved nothing more than seeing a family reunited. The little girls dashed into their mother's skirts for a hug. It had been a rough year for them, having lost their father in a farming accident and having to move to town. They were struggling, it was true, but they had love. They had each other. She hoped their fortune would turn around too. They deserved that. "Have a good afternoon, Collins family. I hope to see you girls on Monday."

"Yes," Mrs. Collins agreed, ushering her children deeper into the house. "A blizzard's winding up for sure. Be safe getting home, Miss Shalvis."

"No worries. Goodbye." She spun around, taking Evie with her. She glanced sideways at the child, who trudged along in the deep snow with her head down, her teeth clenched tight to keep them from chattering. The girl took one bare hand out of her pocket to swipe snow from her eyes.

Why hadn't she noticed the girl had no mittens? Distressed, Penelope stopped in the road and pulled an extra pair of gloves out of her book bag (she always kept a second pair on hand). "Here, Evie. Why don't you slip these on? They'll be much too big but they'll keep your fingers warm."

Evie studied the gloves, her mouth twisting downward. She shook her head, staring down at a patch on her sleeve.

Penelope's chest twisted in sympathy. "This isn't charity. I care about you, Evie. It's starting to get dangerously cold, so you must have gloves. Please hold out your hands."

Evie reluctantly obeyed. She was more than old enough to put them on herself, but Penelope did the honor. The little girl needed a little care and nurturing. It was a sweet thing, it always was to take care of a child. Any child. They were all so priceless. She tugged the gloves into place, making sure the cuff fit snugly beneath Evie's coat sleeves, leaving no skin exposed. Then she unwound her own scarf and wrapped it around the girl's neck and face, brushing off snow, until she was as protected as could be.

"Okay?" She waited for Evie to nod before rising and taking the child by the hand. "Good. Then let's go track down your uncle. I'm betting he's worrying about you right now. Let's go put his mind at ease."

* * *

He was starting to worry. Nathaniel glanced up from his desk, squinting at the curtain of white that his office window had become. It looked bad out there. He glanced at the clock-- nearly twelve-thirty. His stomach growled, and he set down his pen. Evie must be on her lunch hour, too. Was she worried about the storm? Was she afraid of storms? He didn't know.

That's what bothered him most. That he didn't know his only sister's child because his family had scattered long ago. He hadn't known she'd been neglected and unwanted. But that ended here. Determined, he rose from his desk, recapped his ink bottle and reached for his coat.

Someone knocked at his door, barely audible over the freight-train rumble of the wind whipping around the building. He spotted a woman's faint silhouette through the glass and turned the knob.

Miss Shalvis blew in with a furious wave of snow, bringing a little girl with her by the hand. Evie.

Relief lashed through him. He wrestled the door closed. The girl was nothing but white from head to toe. Probably frozen clean through. He gentled his voice so she wouldn't wince when he spoke to her. "I was just coming to check on you."

Evie stared at the floor and didn't respond.

Miss Penelope Shalvis came to the rescue. She smiled in that compassionate way of hers that was like a new dawn shining and ushered the child by the shoulders toward the red-hot stove. "I knew you'd be worried about her. I'm glad we caught you before you went out. You could have passed right by us on the street, not a foot away, and we never would have known it."

"It's blowing bad out there," he agreed, feeling too tall and too out of his element to know how to help. The pretty schoolteacher had already knelt before the child and was peeling back Evie's ice-driven wraps. The teacher was just as ice-covered. "What about you? Will you be able to get home in this?"

"No problem at all. I live only a few blocks away." She was nothing but ice, shivering and trying not to show it. She worked the end of a scarf loose and began unwinding it. Snow crackled and sifted to the floorboards. "I can't tell you how nice this stove feels. Isn't that right, Evie?"

Evie lifted her gaze to her teacher's face and gave a small, tentative nod.

"Exactly. I bet you're cold all the way to your bones, too. That wind drives the warm right out of a girl." Easy-going and understanding, Penelope chattered away as she removed the scarf.

Her scarf, Nathaniel realized. He shook his head, surprised by her thoughtfulness. Then again, he really wasn't surprised at all. Penelope seemed to be just that kind of lady, and that made him like her more.

Dangerous ground, but there it was. Unexplainable warmth burned in the center of his chest as he watched her work the ice off the buttons on Evie's coat.

"Do you know what I like after a chilly walk in the snow?" Penelope asked the girl.

Evie shook her head once, but the way she watched her teacher said that she was curious to know the answer.

"Hot chocolate. It's my secret, guilty pleasure. My stepmother says chocolate is not good for a lady's complexion or her waistline, but I never paid that any mind. Chocolate is wonderful." Penelope freed the last button. "Sometimes I fix myself a cup after a day of school while I'm alone in the schoolhouse. Do you know what that means?"

Evie shook her head as Penelope helped her out of her coat, which was frozen nearly solid and stiff. Bright red gloves dwarfed her little hands. Likely Penelope's gloves, too. Nathaniel's chest cinched tight, touched by this woman's kindness. Clearly she saw how desperately Evie needed it.

"It means," Penelope continued as she rose. "That I have a small tin in my book bag. As your teacher, I am giving you your first homework assignment. You need to drink an entire cup of hot chocolate so you warm up properly. Perhaps your uncle knows how to make it?"

"I have some experience," he admitted dryly. "But I can run down to the mercantile--"

"No. I insist." Penelope hung Evie's coat on a wall peg before reaching for the snow-covered book bag. "It's my treat."

Nathaniel studied the small tin she held out. Fancy. Flowery. He took it anyway, touched by her generosity. "You look cold, too, Miss Shalvis. Perhaps you'll stay and have a cup of hot chocolate with Evie? That way you can warm up before you head back out in that cold."

"Thank you for the invitation." Penelope bit her bottom lip, as if considering the best way to reject his offer. "But I'd like to get home before it gets worse out there."

And while her words were softly said and Nathaniel expected it, he wasn't prepared for the rush of disappointment. Nor was he prepared for how quickly Evie bowed her head, her shoulders slumped. She gave the smallest, barely audible sigh.

He'd never seen a sadder sight. His protective uncle instincts reared up and he wanted to race across the office and wrap her up in his arms, to reassure and comfort her. But then he remembered what had happened last night when he'd gotten too close to her, and it stopped him.

"Please. It would mean a lot to Evie." He stood there, helpless, as Penelope wavered. She looked amazing in the lamplight, the highlights in her brown hair, shining red and gold. She had a perfect complexion, as smooth as fine silk, and a sweetness to her face that made the center of his chest clench hard.

It probably had been a mistake to ask her to stay, but he didn't regret it when Penelope nodded, and Evie's sad little mouth stopped frowning.

"Perhaps I can stay for just one quick cup." Penelope hung her book bag on a hook by her coat and approached the stove. She tossed him an understanding look. "I appreciate the invitation. I am rather frozen and this heat feels good."

"Then sit down and relax." He grabbed one of the cushioned chairs beside his desk and swung it around for her. "Evie, if you're a little less frozen, would you mind running into the next room and bringing two clean cups from the shelf?"

The girl spun way from the stove, spotted the open doorway and padded out of sight, moving as silently as a prowling kitten. Her brown braids hung down her back, still snow-driven. He resisted the urge to go to her and brush that snow and ice away.

"She's a doll. Just adorable." Penelope whispered, palms held out to absorb the stove's heat. She had slender hands, long and lean, sensitive and caring, and another urge took him over. He wanted to fold them in his and hold them there. Safe.

"You got lucky with her," Penelope was saying. "She's a lovely child."

There he went again, having a hard time hearing her, but he concentrated harder this time and tried not to watch her mouth move and form words. Watching her mouth seemed to be a big part of his problem.

"Yes," he agreed, staring hard at a knothole in the floorboard. "She's a good girl. I think she's been alone. It's hard to reach her."

"I think when you lose a mother, you always feel alone. Or at least a part of you does." Penelope shrugged. "It's something that never really goes away."

"That was my experience, too." The words grated out of his throat.

He hadn't talked about his mother's death in a long time. He'd been young, young enough to need a mother desperately. "I was eight when my mother passed. Evie's age."

"I was twelve." Tears of sorrow and obvious love welled in Penelope's hazel eyes, shimmering with tears and sorrow and obvious love. "I'll never forget that day. The worst of all days."

"Life is never the same after that." Troubled, he glanced toward the doorway where his niece had disappeared, listening for sounds of her. He heard a scrape of a wood chair against the floor and the light pad of her shoes as she stepped onto the seat of the chair. He swallowed hard, remembering what it had been like with his mother ripped from his life, with that aching void where her love had been. Evie was suffering from that pain too.

"Life can't be the same after that," Penelope agreed, swishing closer with the rustle of her skirts. She smelled like vanilla and spring. Her hand landed on his sleeve again in a touch so comforting, his chest squeezed tight and didn't release.

"There is always going to be that loss for her." Penelope glanced toward the doorway too, her voice a whisper but the power of her heart in those words. "But you and I both know that all she needs is love. She has you now, and that is going to help her heal."

"I'm not all that much. I know nothing about kids. Especially girls. Little girls." He swallowed hard, trying to keep down his self-doubts and a fear that kept haunting him. "I want more for her. I don't want it to be the way it was for me. There was no one there after Ma died. Pa fell into a bottle and never came out. He loved her truly, so it was hard to blame him."

"But you were eight. Just a child. You needed him." Penelope's oval face crumpled with understanding. "It's a devastating feeling to realize you are truly alone in the world. My father turned to his work. He buried himself in it, and my sister and I never saw him. It was a form of abandonment, enough that I can imagine what you went through, how alone you must have felt."

"And now Evie, too." He sighed, helpless to change the past. His sister had been gone for at least five years. He didn't know why Evie wasn't with her father. "I can't fix what's happened to her, but I can take good care of her. Not that I know how."

"You'll do fine." The beautiful schoolteacher gleamed up at him with a light of respect in her eyes. "You have the only thing you really need. You love her. The rest will follow."

"That's good to hear." His throat ached with emotion so strong, he had to look away. "But it's not very helpful advice."

"Well, I'm a spinster. I've never been faced with the prospect of raising a child." Her voice lilted with lightness, sweet as a melody, and the most arresting sound of all. "But I've found as a teacher that love and patience are all you really need."

He wasn't so sure about that, but Evie padded silently into the room, two cups held carefully in her hands, as if she were terrified of what would happen if she accidentally dropped them.

Love and patience. Well, he thought with a sigh. That's a start.

CHAPTER THREE

"My hot chocolate making skills are a bit rusty." Humor laced Nathaniel Denby's words as he turned from the pot-bellied stove, two steaming cups in hand. "I make no guarantees, but I did my best."

"I was secretly supervising you." Penelope accepted one of the cups. The mellow, chocolate smell wafted up on the steam and she breathed it in. Yum. "I would have pointed out any mistakes."

"That's good to know." He feigned great relief by wiping imaginary sweat from his forehead. She liked the way dark blue flecks twinkled in his eyes when he grinned. "I'm under a lot of pressure, what with you being a chocolate connoisseur, Miss Shalvis, and with this being my first cup of hot chocolate for Evie. I don't want her to get a bad opinion of me."

Evie blushed slightly as she accepted her cup. Dark brown wisps had worked lose from her braids and fell around her face.

"You could never recover from a bad hot chocolate making experience." Penelope teased, blowing on the liquid to cool it. "You could make a thousand other mistakes and still come back to salvage your reputation, but not when it comes to anything chocolate."

"Why, I hadn't realized so much was at stake." He rescued his previously used coffee cup from the stove, now steaming with cocoa. "That's a lot of pressure. Glad I didn't crack."

"Me, too," Penelope bantered back with a wink. "That wouldn't have been manly, but we wouldn't have told anyone. Right, Evie? We would have kept your embarrassing secret."

The corners of Evie's mouth quirked. She blew on her hot chocolate, breathing in the good aroma as if she couldn't quite believe it was hers to drink. Her blue eyes glimmered like Christmas morning.

"Would you two ladies really embarrass me like that?" Amusement quirked up one side of his mouth, drawing a charming dimple. "Surely you are more well-mannered than that."

"Not me," Penelope teased, taking a rich, chocolate sip. "How about you, Evie?"

Evie shook her head, daring to take the smallest sip. Delight transformed her features. Pink colored her cheeks as she took a bigger sip.

Excellent. Penelope smiled in satisfaction. This might be a big step for the girl, relaxing with her uncle and starting to see that life had gotten better. She was with someone who cared for her.

"Then I'm at your mercy, both of you." He leaned against the wall by the stove.

"Yes, you are, and don't you forget it." Penelope's eyes twinkled at him.

"I suppose I should be on my best behavior then." He took in the sight of his niece sipping her way to the bottom of her cup. Little wisps of hair had begun to dry, standing straight up from the blast of the stove. "Maybe I'll close up shop early and head home? We could stop at the mercantile along the way."

Evie looked up blankly, not understanding her uncle's meaning.

Penelope smiled, taking another healthy sip of the comforting chocolate. "Shopping. One of my favorite pastimes."

"Pastimes?" Nathaniel shook his head as if he was not shocked to hear this. "Why do women think shopping is a hobby?"

"Oh, it's more than a hobby. It's a passion." She scooted over to fish a piece of paper out of her coat pocket. "Here's that list I promised you. It's everything Evie needs for school."

Nathaniel took it with a gentlemanly flourish. "I appreciate this, Miss Shalvis."

"Call me Penelope." When she looked up at him, at the strong lines of his face and the depth of character in his blue eyes, she felt something change. She felt a sense of recognition, one she'd never felt before. Suddenly it was as if she'd known Nathaniel for a long time, as if they'd been friends forever. Definitely strange, but not unpleasant. Not unpleasant at all.

"Well, I should be going." She took another sip from her cup before setting it on the edge of his nearby desk. "I appreciate the hospitality and the good company."

"It was our pleasure, wasn't it, Evie?" Nathaniel waited for his niece to nod before his footsteps knelled across the floor. "Let me get your coat for you."

"Oh, there's no need." She'd already plucked it off the wall peg. "You have Evie to take care of. I'm fine."

"It will only take a moment." The corners of his mouth tipped upward, and his dimples made a return appearance. He took the coat from her grasp and held out the garment for her. "Besides, I've got to earn back your good opinion."

"You never lost it." She knew he was only teasing, that he wanted to keep things light for Evie's sake, but she no longer felt jovial. She felt... affected. Her heart was more open, somehow, than it had been when she'd first walked through his door.

Confused, she turned to slip her arms into the sleeves. She shivered when he settled her coat over her shoulders, stepping so near to her she could feel the warm fan of his breath against the back of her neck.

She didn't know what was happening. She wasn't sure what she felt. A little breathless, a little dazed, she busily buttoned her coat to hide the fact that she was blushing.

"Thank you for seeing Evie safely here." He stepped away, one hand on the doorknob. "It means a lot."

"I was happy to do it." Her fingers fumbled on the last button. She suddenly felt awkward, not at all like herself. She blindly reached for her book bag and found it by feel, clumsily unhooking it from its peg and nearly spilling books all over the floor.

"You nearly forgot this." Nathaniel grabbed her scarf and closed the distance between them. He towered over her to settle the scarf around her neck, so close she could breathe in the warm, pleasantly male scent of his skin and the soap from his shirt.

A little skittle of awareness ribboned through her and her breath caught. "I, uh, thank you."

"No problem." This time he gave her a different smile, a quieter one. Not flashy, no dimples, but centered and unwavering.

Attractive. Very, very attractive. Why hadn't she noticed this about him before? It rattled her. She reached for the end of her scarf and missed. She had to grab for it again.

"I should fetch my horse and sleigh and drive you home." He hesitated by the door. Tall, but not too tall. Well-built, but neither too bulky nor too lanky. He focused his dark blue eyes on her with unexpected intensity. "It doesn't feel right to let a lady walk off in a storm like this. Let me fetch my coat."

"No!" She spoke too fast and too loud. She winced. Oops, that was a little telling. Embarrassed, she hooked her book bag strap over her shoulder. She was befuddled. Utterly and completely befuddled. She hadn't felt like this since she was fifteen years old and had a school-girl crush on Phillip Plimpton III, the most popular boy in school.

Get your head on straight, Penelope, she told herself. She was an affirmed spinster (to the horror of her father). She was a schoolteacher (who should be focused on her student's welfare). In fact, she'd totally and momentarily forgotten about her young charge. That was no way for a proper teacher to behave.

She cleared her throat, lifted her chin and gave Nathaniel a professional smile. "I absolutely do not want you to go to the trouble. You have Evie to look after. That's what is important here."

"Oh." He nodded once and stared down at the tips of his polished boots. He looked relieved--at her refusal or at her explanation, she didn't know which.

It didn't matter, she thought, being stern with herself. Attraction to another man was the last thing on her mind. Didn't that usually lead to trouble and heartache? As Nathaniel opened the door, she hesitated, spinning around to give Evie a reassuring smile and a farewell finger wave before bounding through the door and into the hard gusting wind.

White swirled around her, closing off all sight of the warm, lamp-lit room and of handsome Nathaniel Denby standing in the doorway.

That's for the best, she told herself as she trudged along the landing, but the place in her heart that had changed wasn't so sure. He wasn't easy to get out of her mind as she headed home. Not even the battering winds and brutal cold could steal away the warmth she'd felt when he'd smiled at her.

That couldn't be a good thing.

Or could it?

* * *

It was a relief in some ways that Miss Penelope Shalvis had declined his offer of a ride home. Nathaniel pulled on his warm wool coat, pensive in the near dark office. Only one lamp remained burning, for he'd already put out the others and banked the fire. Without the stove's heat, the room had gone to freezing in a matter of minutes.

"Evie, here, wear my scarf." He snatched it from the wall peg and held it out to her. It pained him how thin and worn her coat was, but even worse was the uncertain, almost frightened look that tensed up her sweet face when she had to step close enough to take the scarf from him.

She retreated back quickly in the shadows and settled the too-big scarf around her neck and face. Such a wee thing, small for her age. The blizzard's wrath might be too strong for her, it might knock her over or blow her away from him. He knew without asking she would not take his hand.

"Hold onto my coat hem," he told her. "The wind is strong. Have you been out in a blizzard before?"

She gave one nod. Just one. Obediently she grabbed hold of his coat, keeping a safe arm's length from him. She still seemed deeply uncomfortable, as if it were still too close. He blew out the remaining lamp, opened the door and led the way into the storm. Ice whipped them hard, and he protected her from the brunt of it the best he could.

They made their way down the stairs to the boardwalk below. Gunderson's Mercantile was just a few doors down. He went slowly to match Evie's much smaller steps. Snow needled his face, striking with wrath. When he spotted the faint glimpse of lamplight windows, he gave thanks. It felt as if they'd walked a mile instead of part of a block.

The bell over the door tinkled a merry welcome as he blew in with a mountain of snow. He wrestled the door closed to find Evie flocked white. She let go of his coat the instant she crossed the threshold. She stared at the floor instead of at him.

"Nathaniel Denby, is that you?" a familiar voice called out from deeper inside the store. Footsteps tapped closer, and the store owner's spinster daughter, Gemma, strolled into sight wearing a brown wool dress. "Why, I can't believe you came by. I was in the back locking up."

"You're closing up early because of the storm." He nodded, feeling awkward as he swept off his hat. Snow fell off the brim. "In truth, I was surprised to find you still open."

"And yet you came anyway." Gemma spotted the silent child near the doorway and the stern look vanished from her face. Softness shone in her eyes. "Who do you have here?"

"This is my niece. Evie, this is Miss Gunderson." He winced, hearing the strain in his voice. He'd been sweet on Gemma once, back in the day, but she'd rejected him for another. That romance hadn't worked out, and they'd never gotten over the awkwardness left behind. It was easier to deal with when they weren't alone. Too bad no one else was shopping in the store. "Evie needs a few things. Would you mind if we shop? We'll be quick."

"Absolutely. Anything for a new customer." Gemma offered a kind smile at the girl. "What can I help you find, Evie?"

Evie shook her head, looking hard at the ground. She didn't seem to think she needed anything.

Well, he'd be happy to help her out. "First of all, she needs school supplies. I have a list. Then she needs new clothes. Especially a thick winter coat."

"I have just the thing. Come with me, Evie. If you trust me, Nathaniel, I'll pick out what she needs." Gemma arched a slender eyebrow at him. "Yes?"

"Yes. Thank you." He couldn't measure the relief he felt. He knew next to nothing about female attire and went into a cold sweat at the thought of helping Evie choose undergarments. He nodded at his niece. "Go on with Gemma."

The girl silently obeyed, disappearing down the aisle toward the back of the store. Gemma's voice droned pleasantly as she spoke with the child. He grabbed a basket and started shopping. He grabbed a few staples--beans, sugar and flour, cornmeal and bacon. He added schoolbooks and a slate to the mix before plopping the basket on the front counter. He waited, listening to hear how much progress Gemma was making with Evie, but she'd gone silent too.

"Nathaniel." Gus Gunderson, Gemma's father, burst out from the side room door, a pencil in hand. "How long have you been waiting? Where is that girl of mine? She knows better than to leave a customer like this."

"She's helping my niece." Regardless of what had happened between him and Gemma, he'd never liked the way her father treated her. "I'm not waiting as much as passing time until they are done."

"I see," Gus growled out, but he didn't sound as if he did. He marched out to the counter, threw open an account book and began emptying Nathaniel's basket, recording each item. "We're supposed to be closed."

"Gemma took pity on me." He shrugged. "It's a good thing. Evie's arrival took me by surprise. Maybe you'd better add a ham and a couple loaves of bread."

"Will do." Gus looked grim as he headed to the bread basket. "It's bad out there. I hope you can get home safe in this storm. You have a ways to go."

"Only a few blocks." Not as far as Penelope, he thought, his mind drifting to thoughts of her. Banished or not, they came full of brightness and beauty. He would never forget her kindness to Evie. He'd never forget the comforting blaze of awareness he'd felt when Penelope had touched his arm.

He'd never felt anything like that before.

Footsteps interrupted his thoughts. He whipped around to see Evie dawdling closer, her gait slow and uncertain as she trailed Gemma into the front of the store. Gemma's arms were filled with all sorts of clothing.

"I think Evie thinks this is too much," she explained as she plopped everything on the wooden counter. "But this is enough."

It was the sympathy in Gemma's eyes that made him nod. He didn't question her judgment. She was excellent at her job. But she'd clearly gotten a good look at Evie's clothes--falling apart, handed down. They would make better rags than clothes.

"Make her put on this coat right now." Gemma handed him a robin's egg blue wool garment, very thick and warm. "I can't stand the thought of her walking out there in what she has on."

"Me either," he assured her, grateful. The problem was Evie. She looked away from him, her face red with emotion--embarrassment or upset, he didn't know.

"Take off your coat, Evie," he said gently.

She shook her head.

"Then let me help you." He hunkered down, ready to reach for her top coat button, but she reared back and wrapped her arms around her middle with all her might. Clearly she did not want to relinquish her coat, even for a pretty one. He wasn't going to fight her on this, not now. He was afraid of pushing her too far, so he set the coat on the counter with her other things.

"Maybe later," Gemma suggested. Tears stood in her eyes as she began to help her father with the tallying.

He blinked hard, because his eyes stung too.

Once his total was added to his account and the purchases wrapped, he scooped them up and headed out into the storm. Evie trailed behind him, the occasional tug on the hem of his coat the only sign that she was back there.

By the time he'd fought his way through the drifts and the wind, he'd felt like he'd walked a hundred miles. He stumbled in the back door of his cozy two-story home, started the fire in the cook stove and set Evie down in front of it with the iron door open so the heat would reach her best.

She'd turned blue. Her lips were blue, her face was blue. Her fingers, when he pulled off Miss Shalvis's gloves, were white. That startled him. He tried to cup them in his hands, to rub them so as to force blood into them, but she jumped out of the chair and retreated into the shadows. Her head hung, as if she were ashamed of herself. He caught the glint of a tear on her cheek.

"I won't try and touch you again," he told her softly. "But you need to be where it's warmest. Come sit back down and hold your hands up to the heat. All right?"

When he retreated, she nodded and settled down into the chair like a ghost. She rubbed away her tears with the back of her tattered dress sleeve.

He was dying inside. He didn't know what had happened to Evie, but he should have asked more questions of her uncle. He should have demanded them. But he'd been too shocked and taken aback by the man's callousness when he'd shoved the child at him, leaving her behind. The man had hopped back on his horse and dashed away before Nathaniel could protest.

Hands trembling, he set a kettle of water on the stove to heat. Evie didn't move. She sat so still it was hard to tell if she was breathing. He thought of his little sister. She'd looked a lot like that, with dark brown braids and big blue eyes. His chest ached with a combination of loss and regret and devotion. This was his sister's child. Clearly Evie hadn't had the life his sister would have wanted for her.

But that would change. He would make sure of it, or he'd die trying. His hands fisted with resolve and something crackled against his palm. Penelope's gloves. They were frozen solid, shot with ice, but they reminded him of her.

She was a gifted teacher. She had a way with children. It was plain to anyone. He hung the gloves up to thaw, mulling over an idea. He was a bachelor. Nearly every one of his close friends were bachelors. It wasn't as if he could go to them for advice.

But Penelope knew children. Relieved, he glanced over his shoulder at the girl who seemed more of a shadow than a real child. The growing fire cast cheerful orange and red light over her.

His mind mulling, he unwrapped his purchases. He took out the fresh loaves of bread, beans and sugar. He found the ham Gus had wrapped. It looked like supper would be easy. He peered up to see Evie had found the broom and was sweeping the floor with careful skill. He thought about reprimanding her, this wasn't the first time she'd silently started doing chores, but he didn't want to make her upset. His chest ached for her. She looked so spindly as she swept. Bones poked against the back of her dress, making little knobs down her back.

Yes, she would get a big plate full of food tonight. He'd make sure of that. Upset, he tugged too hard on the brown wrapping paper and soft folds of red and blue flannel tumbled onto the tabletop. Evie's new dresses. He blew out a breath, troubled. There was just no other word for it. Feeding her and clothing her properly was just the start.

Evie's heart had been broken. He didn't know how to begin fixing that, but he'd find a way. Miss Penelope Shalvis would know exactly how to help.

CHAPTER FOUR

Penelope wasn't sure what had pulled her out of her book, but she blinked, the words of *Persuasion* blurred on the page as the room came into focus around her. Her little rental cottage wasn't much by her parent's standards back home in Boston, but she'd grown to love the charming place. Just four rooms, and that was more than she needed. The soft yellow flowers on the wallpaper added cheer on this chilly afternoon.

She yawned, covering her mouth with one hand. Something was different, she realized right away. The winds had died. The snow had stopped. Finally. The blizzard was over.

She snapped her book shut and sat up straight on the sofa. Lemony sunshine fought its way through the clouds to glint on her front window. Boy, did that feel good after two days of being shut in her house with nothing but the gray twilight of the storm to keep her company. She dropped her book on the cushion, bounded to her feet and skipped to the window.

Doors were opening on a few of the houses across the street. A couple of kids tumbled out into the high drifts, their excited voices echoing in the stillness. She wished she was a kid again so she could do the same thing--holler and shout and slide down the steep side of a drift and crash into the snow below.

Just think what the good townspeople of Bluebell would say if she gave in to that whim! Smiling to herself--and imagining climbing up the backside of an eight foot drift, dropping onto her bottom and giving a mighty push to go sledding--she gave a little sigh. She could almost feel the kiss of the icy air on her face, the exhilaration as she gained speed down the slope and the world around her blurring as she slid faster and faster.

A bold knock rapped at her front door.

Probably one of her students come to ask if there would be school tomorrow, she thought, spinning on her heels and sailing across the floor. Whoever it was knocked again, impatient as she grabbed her wool shawl from the wall peg and shouldered it on.

"Coming!" She called out gaily, grabbing the knob. "Sadie Gray, is that you knocking at my door?"

But the instant the door swung open, the tall, wide-shouldered shadow towering on her doorstep told her she could not be more wrong. Every nerve ending she had snapped to attention.

"Miss Shalvis." Nathaniel Denby tipped his hat cordially. "Good afternoon."

"Good afternoon to you, Mr. Denby and Evie." She caught sight of the waif hovering in the middle of the snowy yard, wearing her ragged coat and a blue and black striped scarf--clearly her uncle's. She smiled at the child, although it was the man who held her attention. "To what do I owe this pleasure?"

"You left a few things at my office." His solemn blue eyes met hers, belying the light tone of his voice and the quirk of a friendly smile on his lips. Burdens were shadowed there, dark and deep. "Evie wanted to make sure you got them as soon as the storm was over."

"And indeed, you must have bolted out the door to come see me the instant the snow stopped falling." Penelope turned her attention to the child standing uncertainly in knee-deep snow. Her ragged, faded brown dress was wet and snow caked, but she didn't seem to notice as she trudged slowly forward, head down. There seemed to be no change in the child's sad state.

No wonder Nathaniel seemed upset.

"You are a very thoughtful girl." She wanted to kneel down, wrap her arms about the child and hug her so tightly she chased away every bit of sadness, but she sensed Evie wasn't ready for that. She accepted the pair of gloves (freshly laundered by the looks of it) and the hot chocolate tin. "Thank you so much, Evie. Would you please come in?

I've been stuck in this house all alone, and I would love some company."

Evie bit her bottom lip, unsure but tempted.

"I had promised Evie she could play in the snow while there's still daylight." Nathaniel explained. "Maybe you would like to come out with us and stretch your legs?"

Tempting, so tempting. Penelope breathed in the fresh air, holding that chill deep in her lungs. The crisp, clean scent of snow, the wintry wind tinged with wood smoke and the smell of mountain peaks made her smile. She loved the kiss of the light breeze against her cheeks. The part of her she always kept carefully contained (she was a prim and proper schoolteacher, you know) yearned to be set free.

But there was the slight problem of Nathaniel Denby--or, rather, her reaction to him. A reaction she was trying to ignore (which did no good). Her nerve endings kept snapping like a bowstring drawn too tight and then released. Not to mention she couldn't stop smiling as he arched an eyebrow at her, causing pleasant, attractive crinkles around his eyes. Really attractive.

"Come on." He gestured toward the road. "Evie and I will make sure you stay out of trouble. Right, Evie?"

Evie nodded, her dark blue eyes lighting with a rare hope.

Impossible to disappoint the child and, honestly, she did want to stretch her legs. She shook her head at Nathaniel--poor unsuspecting Nathaniel. "Oh, you think you can keep me out of trouble, do you? You don't know what you're getting into."

"You're the town schoolteacher. You're a proper lady from Boston." He held up his hands, palms up. "How much trouble can you be?"

"That just goes to show you know nothing about girls." She shrugged out of her shawl and reached for her warmest coat. "Poor you, Evie. However do you put up with this guy?"

Evie shrugged. The corners of her mouth hooked up a smidgeon.

So, the girl had a sense of humor. That was promising. Penelope poked her arms into her sleeves and caught her breath when Nathaniel leaned in to help her with her coat. He'd done it before back in his office, but then her heart hadn't seized up like this. Now her lungs went tight and a little bit of *wow* settled into her chest.

She gazed up at the man, taking in the details she hadn't noticed before. The small cleft in his chin was perfectly carved, balancing his strong face. His spectacles framed his blue eyes just right, magnifying the kindness in them. When he looked at her, she could see his steadfastness. Her pulse kicked up a pace because she liked the way his smile spread slowly across his mouth, transforming the lines of his face and settling in his gaze. He seemed to smile with every part of him, eyes, heart and soul, and a little sigh escaped her.

Did she like Nathaniel Denby--you know, like *that?* Fascinated, she stepped back, her palms damp as she pulled on her gloves.

"Poor Evie is right. I'm hard to put up with." His sleeve brushing her shoulder as he closed the door. "She was probably suffering during that blizzard, cooped up in the house with me. Isn't that right, Evie?"

Evie stared at the too-large pair of men's driving gloves on her hands.

"Men are very trying." Penelope breezed into the sunlight, absorbing its cheerfulness as she plunged through the deep snow in her front yard. "I should know. I had four difficult stepbrothers and an overbearing father. Even my fiancé was taxing."

"Fiancé?" Nathaniel missed a step and nearly plunged face-first into the snow. "You have a fiancé?"

"Had. Past tense. But I gave him his ring back and broke free just in time. It was a close call." She waltzed along as if her broken engagement hadn't hurt at all, as if it were the very best thing that could have happened. Her skirts swished and swirled with her gait, and her tailored coat cinched in at her tiny waist, giving her an elegant look.

"You must have crushed the poor fellow." He cleared his throat, but his voice sounded strained. Maybe because he'd known once or twice how it felt. He'd been crushed by a woman before. Considering his luck and the way he felt about Penelope, it was likely to happen again.

"Me? No, I didn't crush him." Breezily, she waved one slender hand in the air as if to dismiss his concern for that other man. "He's the one who crushed me."

"Really?" Now he was curious. He caught up beside her in the snow. His heart lurched in his chest, far too sympathetic to her and way too interested. Wisely, he struggled to hold his feelings steady. "That's why I never get too involved in a relationship. Feelings get hurt. Hearts get crushed."

"Smart." Penelope narrowed her eyes at him, as if she were trying to figure him out.

"Hey! Evie!" A little girl's voice called out from the street.

"Sadie! I'm not surprised you're out playing in the snow already." Penelope waved at the approaching child. "My stepbrothers used to have a toboggan like that. I would steal it from them and go down the hill on our property as fast as the wind."

"This one'll go real fast, too." Sadie was adorable in her trousers and wool coat and purple knit hat, scarf and mittens. "Evie, do you wanna come, too? I'll let you ride it and everything."

Evie studied the toboggan for a long moment. It was easy to read the longing on her face. Nathaniel wondered when last Evie had been allowed to play. His ribs felt tight with gratitude to Sadie Gray and her friendly offer.

"Go ahead and have fun, Evie." That's what he wanted for her.

Her surprised smile was reward enough. It was easy to see her thankfulness. She fell in stride with Sadie and the two girls scampered off down the street, the toboggan leaving a trail in the snow behind them.

"Well, it looks as if my pairing was the right one." Penelope beamed with satisfaction, watching the girls head down the road. "I almost set her with Ida, but Ida is a quiet girl, too. Look how she and Sadie are already fast friends."

"That's what Evie needs. A friend." The word caught in his throat right along with the gratitude. He didn't know what it was about Penelope that made him feel so much--but he owed her for helping his niece. "Thank you for all you've done for her."

"I haven't done that much. You're the one who took her in and gave her a home." Penelope's rich hazel eyes fastened on his, full of swirls of color--threads of copper, brown, green and yellow. "How is that going?"

"That's another reason I came by." He plunged his fists into his coat pocket, not sure where to start. "I don't have family to turn to. My friends are as clueless about kids as I am. I need some advice, and you're the best person I can think of to ask."

"Me? I'm afraid I don't know much." She sparkled up at him, light and sweet, kneeling down to grab a handful of pristine, sugary snow. It sparkled, shot with diamonds in her hand where the sun found it. "My stepmother was always chiding me because I spent too much time with my nose in a book instead of being out in the real world."

"You might be asking the wrong person, because I don't see

anything wrong with keeping your nose in a book." His throat felt tight and a powerful longing nestled deep within him, the urge to reach out and take hold of her hand. To cradle it, to hold it with reverence. It was a desire he could not give in to. "I read all the time. I'm not as interested in the real world as I am in a good book."

"I know what you mean. There's nothing like getting lost in those pages and swept away to another place and time." She closed her fist over the snow in her hand. "What kind of advice do you need?"

"It's about Evie. But you've already guessed that, haven't you?"

"True. She's such a sad little girl. Your heart must be breaking for her." Penelope sighed, coming to a stop at the edge of the street. She caught sight of the girl alongside Sadie, the two making their way down the lane to where several boys were tobogganing from the peak of a stable's roof. A snowdrift nestled up alongside the building, making one long slope. "It must be hard not knowing what has happened to her."

"She's been shut up in the house with me through the storm, and she still hasn't said one word." His throat worked. His voice sounded tight. Unmistakable concern lined his face. "I don't know what to do for her. I don't know how to make her open up."

"Something tells me you're already doing everything right." She had no doubt. Nathaniel Denby had a good heart. She'd never forget the sight of him standing outside the schoolyard in the storm, unable to walk away and leave Evie behind. "Love is really all that she needs."

His throat worked, like he was mulling that piece of advice over. "I bought her a new winter coat. She refuses to wear it. I bought her half a dozen new dresses. She won't touch them. I don't know what to do about that."

"Neither do I." Penelope stared down at the snow in her hand, taking a moment to mold it into a small ball. She cast a sidelong glance down the street to where Evie stood at the back of a line of children, waiting for their turn at the stable roof. Sadie chattered away beside her. "Maybe she just needs time to see that everything is going to be all right."

"You were a teacher before you came here to Bluebell, right?" He sounded troubled. He sounded like a man determined to help his niece, but who feared he couldn't.

He cared so much. She liked him even more for that. "You're

wondering if I've ever come across a student like Evie before."

"Yes." Relief lined his face. "She doesn't talk. That can't be normal. I thought about asking Doc Hartwell, but I don't want to hear what he's going to say."

"Why not?"

"Because she's afraid of me." His throat worked as he stopped walking to stare down the street where Evie nodded in response to whatever Sadie had said to her. "She shrinks away whenever I get close. She does chores without being asked and gets upset when I tell her to stop. She's half-starved, that's plain to see. I don't know how long she's been treated like this. What if it's--"

He didn't finish, but he didn't need to.

"It won't be permanent." She assured him. "Look how she responds to the other children. She's smiling at Sadie. I really think she just needs time to see that she can trust you. She just needs to learn that she will be safe, that's all, and her life is going to be better here with you."

"How do I show her that? I want to make her life better now." He set his fine shoulders. "Tell me you have all the answers."

"I wish. I taught only one term back in Boston, much to my parent's horror." She took a step forward into the bright snow, letting the sun's glare spill over her. It felt right, utterly natural, when he stayed at her side.

"Just one term?" He sounded surprised. "I don't know why I thought you'd been teaching a long time."

"It's my age. I'm twenty-three. A spinster by society's standards, and embarrassingly so for my parents." She gave a self-conscious shrug. The path she was following rose up into a hard-packed drift, a little slick beneath her shoes.

"Why embarrassingly so?" Nathaniel's hand shot out to clasp her elbow, keeping her steady on the incline. "Although I am shocked no man has snatched you up, especially in this town."

"There are a lot of men compared to women here," she agreed, squinting as the sun blinded her. "But I broke off my engagement last September. I'm not looking for any romantic entanglements just yet."

"What happened?" he asked kindly.

It was that note of kindness that got to her, that broke down her resolve. She hadn't talked to anyone about what had really happened with Alexander, not even her close friends. "I fell in complete love for the first time in my life. He worked in the accounting office of my father's shipping business."

"First love can be powerful." He nodded with sympathy, his grip on her elbow steady and reassuring. He came to a stop at the top of the drift. They towered over the street by a good eight feet. "For me it was Minnie Abernathy."

"Minnie was the first girl to break your heart?" She tilted her head, studying him intently. "Or did you do the breaking?"

"Me? I assure you, I've never broken a lady's heart. Not ever." He adjusted his Stetson, drawing it down to block the slanting sun. "If a lady were to love me truly, I would love her without end forever."

"Spoken like a true dandy." She seemed to notice the snowball in her hand and glanced at it, then at him with calculation. "I can't believe I let you draw me in like that. Here I thought you were a sincere man."

"I am sincere, or I try to be." He laughed at that, at the idea of him being a lady's man, playing with a woman's heartstrings. "Minnie did the breaking. After six months of what I thought was courtship, she told me it was nice having me for a friend, but she'd started dating someone she could be serious about."

"Ouch." She winced in sympathy. "Was the friendship thing news to you?"

"It was. It started a sad pattern of relationships for me that I won't bore you with." He squared his shoulders, choosing to keep his woeful attempts at courting secret from her or she would start to agree with those ladies who'd passed him by. He couldn't bear the thought of that just yet. "I know I'm not an exciting man. I sit at a desk working all day, and when I'm done, I read a book for excitement."

"Hey, books are great excitement." Her rosy mouth smiled around those words and he blinked, stunned by the overpowering urge to kiss her. To just plant his lips on hers and wrap her tight in his arms, hold her against his chest and kiss her until the world ended or she pushed him away--whichever came first.

"You still haven't told me what happened." He cleared his throat, trying to sound unaffected, like a man who was just making conversation, but his pulse drummed in his veins. He wanted to know.

"Alexander seemed like the perfect man for me. My father approved of him. My stepmother adored him." She stared off down the street where Evie and Sadie were on the peak of the barn's roof, carefully crawling onto the toboggan two of the bigger schoolboys held steady for them. Penelope's oval face tightened with sorrow. "I'd watched all my friends fall in love and marry. My sister was already married and a mother. My cousins were all married. I was the lone spinster, with everyone whispering behind my back how they feared I would never marry, not now that the bloom of my youth is gone."

"You're still a lovely bloom to me." The words were out before he could stop them, and he grimaced. He'd learned a long time ago in his failed attempts at beauing ladies that a man could not speak his heart plainly. It made him look like a sappy dolt.

Tears rose in Penelope's eyes, and she turned to him. It was gratitude shining there, touching her smile, framing her face and sounding wobbly in her voice. "Thank you for saying that. It's not true, I know, but that was kind of you, Nathaniel."

He heard the pain in her voice, a hurt he didn't understand, but he couldn't help wanting to make it better for her. "You're incredibly lovely, Penelope. Anyone who doesn't think so has something wrong with them."

"Well, funny you should say that." She bit her bottom lip, staring down at the snowball still clutched in one hand. "I was so desperate to be loved that I didn't see what Alexander was doing. Now that you know the truth about me, you're sorry you asked, right?"

"No." There he went, being honest again, but he didn't know how else to be. A more dashing man might know how to lay on the charm, how to use her confession to his advantage. He didn't have those skills. "I'm sorry you went through that. It's only human what you feel. We all want to be loved. We all want to love."

"Yes." She blinked against those tears, still pooled in her eyes. They shimmered but they did not fall. "I didn't see the truth about Alexander. I fell for him deeply. I thought we were a perfect match, that we were alike. He seemed to treasure me. I thought I'd found everything I'd ever wanted."

"How did you find out the truth?" His chest tightened, already aching for her.

"I overheard him the night of our engagement party, talking to one of his old friends." Agony carved sad lines around her eyes. "I went to knock on the library door to tell him the first of the guests had pulled up in their carriage, but the door was ajar. I could hear the conversation within."

She paused, taking a gulp of air. The sun brightened, finding her as if with a loving hand. He had to fight every instinct he had not to reach out and draw her into his arms. With one hand on her elbow, he could feel her muscles tense. He could feel her pain.

Whoever Alexander was, Nathaniel hated him for that.

"Alexander and his best friend were laughing about what a fool I was." She said the words quietly, holding herself very still. "Alexander confessed how easy I had been to dupe, how I ate up his praise and his lies like candy. That he'd already talked to my father and would be appointed vice president of the company upon our marriage. That was why he'd courted me. He saw an opportunity to advance himself, and he took it. Marrying me would have made him rich. That's all he cared about."

"That had to have been devastating." He imagined an elaborate party, guests arriving to celebrate her engagement. "What did you do?"

"I did nothing at first. I went along with the charade." She worked the snowball in her hand again, rounding the corners, her voice trembling. "But when I confronted Alexander privately later, he denied it. He tried to pass it off as a joke between old friends. But I knew better. He even talked to my father about it, so when I broke off the engagement my parents were on his side. Not only was I humiliated, but my father gave me an ultimatum. I had to marry Alexander or I would be disowned and disinherited."

"So you came here to teach school instead." Nathaniel hurt for her. His father had failed as a father, but it hadn't been by choice. He hadn't abandoned his children deliberately. "What you did took a lot of strength."

"Oh, I don't know about that. I took the first teaching job I could find, and I'm glad I did. Look how well my life is turning out." She beamed, luminous with the sunshine gracing her, shining through her pain. She glanced down the street. "Wow. Look at Evie and Sadie go! That slope is really fast. Oh, Nathaniel, Evie's laughing."

"She is." His throat closed up, watching the little girl roll off the toboggan at the bottom and tumble into the snow. It was too far away to hear her laughter, but he could see it.

"That looks like so much fun." Penelope tossed the snowball at him, hitting his hat brim. His Stetson flew off, cart wheeling down the drift's slope in front of him. She shrugged. "Oops. Sorry about that."

"I don't think you are." He moved without thinking, hauling her to him as he stepped off the peak of the drift. Down they want, skidding on their shoes, losing balance and landing on their backsides, gliding all the while down the drift made icy by the sun's touch. Her laughter mixed with his as they spun in a fast circle, round and round until they came to a breathless stop on the street below.

CHAPTER FIVE

Penelope blinked. Even though she'd stopped moving and she was bottom down on the snow, her head still spun. Maybe it was the exhilaration of sliding fast down the steep drift, or maybe it was the man.

"You're in big trouble now," she informed Nathaniel, who was still sprawled in the snow. "If you think you can push me down that slope and get away with it--"

"I didn't push you. I, er, fell."

"A likely story. You could have let go of me, but you didn't." She grabbed a handful of snow and started packing it. "You took me with you. There will be consequences for this. I can't let you go unpunished."

"Why not?" He arched an eyebrow, giving him a dashing look despite his boy-next-door, scholarly appearance. He squinted at her through his spectacles. "I'm a good guy. You could show me leniency."

"I don't approve of leniency. At least not for you." She gave the snowball a final pat and aimed, sending it arcing toward him.

"Why not for me?" He ducked just in time, so the icy ball winged by him, brushing the outside curve of his shoulder.

"Because who knows when you might do it again? You're unrepentant." She bounced to her feet, already packing another snow weapon. "No, it might set a dangerous precedent."

He bounded to his feet too, scooping one hand into the loose snow at his feet. "Are you afraid I might spot you in town, run over and haul you off the boardwalk into the snow?"

"You seem like the type." Laughing now, she gave a squeal as he aimed and gave his snowball a practiced toss. She ducked but not fast enough. It grazed her arm. A fine spray of snow rained across her face.

"Now you are in trouble, Mr. Denby." She rushed toward him, arm poised for the perfect throw. She could feel the power in her muscles and the trueness of her aim as the snowball left her hand.

It arced perfectly toward him, dead center at his chest. He turned, he tried to outrun it but it slammed into his left shoulder blade.

"Oops. That may have hit harder than I intended," she confessed. "I don't know my own strength."

"That's no excuse." He filled his hands with snow as he rushed toward her. Running fast, surprisingly fast. "Remember, you started this."

"I see you are like many men I know." She was laughing too hard to really run, but her feet did manage to propel her up another drift where she threw a fast snowball at him, hoping to hold off his attack. "Quick to avoid blame and any wrongdoing."

"Yes. That's me. I avoid responsibility, too. And I don't mind pelting women with snowballs." He charged up the drift behind her, gaining ground.

She knelt to grab more snow, but it was all too icy on this side of the drift where the wind had packed it. Weaponless, she skidded to a stop at the crest of the drift. "You wouldn't hit an unarmed woman, would you?"

"Yes." He drew back his arm to bombard her with the enormous, deadly looking snowball, but instead he grabbed her by the arm with his other hand and they skidded over the edge of the enormous drift together.

Down, down, down they skated on the soles of their shoes, wobbling to keep their balance. When she almost fell, it was his strong grip that held her upright, his strength that saw her safely to the bottom where they stopped together, face to face, and his arms came around her waist.

"Whoa there," he said, his baritone rumbling deep and pleasant.

So, so pleasant. It seemed to pervade her body, to spill into her blood and rush through her with a cozy breathlessness. She tingled everywhere, glittering as bright as the diamond flecks on the sun swept snow. She laughed, tilted her head back and their gazes met.

Locked.

Her heart skidded to a stop, forgetting to beat. Everything within her stilled as Nathaniel's indigo blue gaze darkened to a dizzying near-black. She saw his heart there, honorable and true. The world around her silenced until there was only the two of them graced by the sun, surrounded by the white perfection of snow. In that endless moment, she stood caught by the power of his gaze and the tenderness there as he leaned in, slanted his mouth over hers and brushed her with a flawless kiss.

Amazing. That was the only word that came to mind. His lips were soft but firm--not mushy, the way Alexander's had been. This kiss was enchanting--not uncomfortable or too sloppy and wet. No, she thought as her toes curled and her eyes drifted shut. This was a fairytale kiss, the kind she read about in her books. It was real, after all. Not fiction.

And it was happening to her.

"Uh, goodness," a woman's startled voice sounded very close by. "Excuse me, I don't mean to interrupt. Maybe I'd better come back inside, Josslyn, and leave these two to their kissing."

"Oh, my yes. That sounds like a good idea!" another woman's voice answered quite merrily.

Penelope knew she should step back and break both the kiss and Nathaniel's hold on her, but her lips were too happy. Her brain was too dazed to give the command. Nathaniel did the gentlemanly thing and did it for her, lifting his mouth from hers, ending their kiss and the sweet fiery tenderness. His arms loosened, falling away from her waist, freeing her. She stood there, wobbling slightly, trying to collect her thoughts.

The McPhee sisters' aunt, Aumaleigh, stood on the doorstep of the nearby cottage, smiling merrily. Her bluebonnet blue eyes glittered with amusement. "I remember kissing a young man like that once. I was engaged to him."

"Personally, I am quite scandalized by this display." Josslyn, Aumaleigh's cook at the Rocking M Ranch, winked saucily. "What a way for a schoolteacher to behave. And Nathaniel. Good to know you don't waste any time."

"I, uh, apologize for being so ungentlemanly." He'd turned red to the tips of his ears. "Miss Shalvis, perhaps I'd better escort you home."

"Yes indeed." Her face felt hot. Her nose was glowing strawberry-red. She could see it when she crossed her eyes.

But the older women didn't look terribly scandalized--far from it. Aumaleigh McPhee, stately and lovely in her dove-gray winter coat and dark blue hat, smiled at her hopefully. She wore middle age well. Her thick, molasses-dark hair framed her heart-shaped face with the luster of a younger woman.

"No need for you two to be embarrassed," Aumaleigh said easily as she adjusted her scarf. "Love seems to be in the air lately. Josslyn, I'll see you later now that the kissing seems done. Penelope, you have a nice time with your beau."

"Have a lovely afternoon, Aumaleigh." Penelope could hear the strain in her voice. Clearing her throat didn't chase away the thick, lump of emotion lodged there. Did she want to be kissing Nathaniel Denby? Moreover, did she want to be seen kissing him?

As Josslyn gave them a goodbye wave before closing her door and Aumaleigh gracefully crossed the walk to her waiting mare and sleigh parked alongside the street, Penelope didn't know what to say. Her lips buzzed with the memory of that kiss--that extraordinary, superlative, unexpected kiss. Did Nathaniel feel the same way?

"Sorry about that." He plunged his hands into his coat pockets, staring hard at the snowy tips of his boots. "Guess I was caught up in the moment."

"Oh." That sounded like a no. It must have been just an ordinary kiss for him. Disappointment roared through her like a blizzard, freezing her to the core. That rise of hope, that excited feeling of maybe--of what might come from this moment--died away. The sun chose that moment to hide behind a bank of clouds, casting shadows across them. The sparkles faded from the snow. The brightness faded from the day, leaving only gray.

Yes, Penelope thought, that's just how she felt. She took a slow step to match Nathaniel's, pausing when he knelt to scoop up his hat. They were headed back to her house, just a few doorsteps away. They trekked up the drifts and back down again. There was no sliding, no slipping, no snowball throwing.

Just silence. She listened to the scrunching sound of her shoes in the snow, feeling a heaviness fill her chest with every step she took. The happy, ringing laughter of children playing echoed in her head, at odds with the solemn stillness that had fallen between her and Nathaniel.

"I suppose that kiss wasn't very good for your reputation as the schoolteacher." He finally broke the silence, his tone low and hollow. Regret carved lines into his face. "I'm sorry if I was out of line."

"No, I should have kept my head. I don't know what happened to my common sense." She only now thought of the strict contract she'd signed with the superintendent. "I have a strict morality clause. I can't remember what it said at this very moment, my mind seems to be blank, but I'm sure it forbids public shows of any, uh, affection."

She had to look away from him, her face heating again. Clearly there had been no affection on his part. She climbed her front steps, lifting her skirts so she wouldn't trip on them in the deep snow. That heaviness in her chest increased, becoming a big block of iron sitting there, refusing to let her breathe.

"If you have any problems from this, I'll handle it for you. For free." His voice deepened, professional now, the lawyer and not the man. "It's the least I can do, considering I lost my head for a moment there, too."

"Right. We were both just caught up in the moment." Her voice trembled, and that shamed her. Why couldn't she be a more sophisticated type of woman, worldly and polished, the kind of lady who could dismiss a kiss handily, who could waltz up the stairs and into her house without almost tripping on her own feet? If only she could be the kind of woman who was in total control of her heart. Miserably, she reached for her doorknob.

Nathaniel was there first, leaning in, the press of his arm like warm steel against her shoulder. He turned the knob and opened the door for her. "I hope this doesn't change anything between us."

"You mean with Evie?" She swept past him, her slender back straight and her chin up, her skits rustling around her as she spun around in the little entry way to face him. "Of course I will continue to help her. I'm her teacher."

"I just don't want you to be uncomfortable." He felt awkward standing on the doorstep with the memory of her lips on his. The truth was, if Aumaleigh hadn't burst out of Josslyn's house, then he would probably still be kissing her and holding her tight against his chest, safe in his arms. The tenderness he'd felt in that moment remained, tenaciously rooted in his heart. "I'm sorry for kissing you."

"Oh." She hung her head, as if trying to hide the wince that traveled across her beautiful face. Was she disappointed in his apology? "I'm sure we can move on past this."

When she raised her chin, she gave no hint of emotion away on her face. She was once again the professional, polished schoolteacher, but her eyes were sad.

And so was he. He took a step back. "Thank you, Miss Shalvis. Have a good afternoon."

"You too." She nodded politely, unaware of the bits of snow clinging to her lustrous hair, sparkling in the lamplight. She looked like a storybook princess from some faraway land, and his chest twisted painfully with a fierce longing he could not explain.

He did the sensible thing. He took a step back, tipped his hat in farewell and walked away while he still had something left of his heart.

* * *

Aumaleigh McPhee shook out the buffalo robe, spread it over her lap. Her mare Buttons lifted her head, at the ready. Aumaleigh gathered the reins, shook them and the sleigh jerked to a start, zipping down the lane as Buttons gained speed.

Call her nosy, but she couldn't help glancing over at Penelope's little bungalow. Nathaniel Denby was walking away from Penelope's door after seeing her home. Wasn't that interesting? Why hadn't he stayed for tea or something? A man couldn't beau a lady if he didn't spend time with her. She drew Buttons to a stop.

"Nathaniel!" She leaned over the sleigh's front seat to smile at the young man. "Where are you off to in such a hurry?"

"I have to fetch my young niece." He came to a halt next to her sleigh. "She's living with me now."

"Oh, is that so?" She hadn't heard, and she liked to think she was up on most of the news in this town. "Which one is she? Wait, is she the little brunette with Sadie Gray?"

"More like the one getting into trouble with Sadie Gray." He had a wry sense of humor. "I think they are building snow berms over Mrs. Crabtree's front windows."

"Mrs. Crabtree probably deserves it." Aumaleigh risked a glance down the street. Yes, indeed, several children were packing snow against the front of the cantankerous lady's house. "If you are wise, you'll fetch your niece before chaos ensues."

"That's my thought exactly, although it's nice to see her with friends." His forehead furrowed in thought, drawing deep grooves of concern. "That's why I was speaking with Miss Shalvis. She's offered to help with my niece."

"Help? I don't think so. You can't fool me, Nathaniel. I know what I saw." She said the words kindly, because she remembered how tender those new feelings of love could be and how vulnerable it made a person. Recollections of her own youth and her one great love flooded her. Yes, indeed, love made the heart vulnerable. "Penelope is a good match for you. How long have you been beauing her?"

"I'm not beauing her." Nathaniel straightened his shoulders. "We were just out for a walk."

"It looked to me to be a great deal more than that." Aumaleigh might not be an expert when it came to romance (she'd been a spinster for so many years she'd lost count), but she could see the look of love on the man's face--and the sadness too. Something hadn't gone smoothly. "You should ask her out for a walk more often. Think about it."

He didn't seem to know how to answer. Instead he thumbed his spectacles higher on his nose, looking a bit puzzled. Well, men were often puzzled over romantic things. He would figure it out. She nodded. "Have a good afternoon, Nathaniel."

"You too, Aumaleigh." He tipped his hat. Such a polite young man he was. Smiling, she sped away.

My, it sure looks as if things between him and Penelope had progressed quickly, if they were kissing already! Aumaleigh smiled to herself, reining Buttons right at the intersection and heading through the residential streets to the town's main thoroughfare. How times had changed. Back in her day, it would have been appalling if you allowed a beau to kiss you. That was only appropriate if a couple was engaged.

Amused, she leaned back in the seat, her attention drifting, remembering her first kiss. It had been only moments after Gabriel Daniels had proposed to her. Oh, what a sweet kiss that had been. Like fine wine--rich and cozy with a hint of fire and a delight that lingered long after the kiss was done. She'd been transported by that kiss, her heart in rapture, her soul complete.

That had been a lifetime ago, she thought with regret.

Their love had not withstood the test of time--not on his side, anyway. But when she looked up and realized she'd gone down the very street she'd been avoiding for weeks, she mentally scolded herself and nearly turned the sleigh around. But that was silly.

Sure, Gabriel Daniels had come to town with his family for the holidays and had stayed on for a few weeks. So far she'd managed to avoid a face-to-face confrontation with him. There was no reason to think she would run into him now. Gabriel might be staying in his nephew's house, but what were the chances he would be staring out the front window at the exact moment she would be driving by?

Slim to none, that's what. She lifted her chin to reassure herself. She would be fine. Nothing was going to happen.

Besides, even if he *did* see her through the window, it wouldn't matter. She would be gone down the street by the time he made it to the door. But even the thought of seeing him in person made her heartbeat slam wildly against her ribcage. Just to be safe, she urged Buttons into a fast trot as the house came into sight. She caught a glimpse of lamp-lit windows, but that was all as she dashed by.

See? There'd been nothing to worry about. Relieved, she reined her mare onto Main Street and tried to ignore her extremely damp palms and the bead of sweat rolling down her forehead. Having to look him in the face would have been too painful. She'd gotten through all these decades by not thinking about him and those long ago broken dreams she'd had once, fantasizing about being Gabriel's wife and of cradling their newborn child in her arms.

Main Street was busy. Folks had ventured out to run their errands and do their grocery shopping. The mercantile looked like a madhouse--she'd have to drop by and grab a few items at another time. There wasn't a parking spot in the entire block. Vivian Gunderson, out for a walk, called out her name and waved her cane. Aumaleigh called back warmly to the elderly woman and continued on her way. There were others to greet and wave to as she passed the next block. She just wanted to get home without running into anything or anyone Gabriel related (what if he was out shopping, for instance?).

But one sight drew her to a stop. Her nieces were standing on the boardwalk in front of a vacant storefront, all five of them, arguing with one another. Strawberry blond Iris, the oldest, had turned red with anger.

"How could you do this?" she demanded. Sweet, introverted Iris gave an uncharacteristic huff. "All on your own. Without telling us. For weeks. *Weeks!*"

"I, for one, am shocked." Blond and quirky Magnolia gave a mischievous wink. "You should have told me first. I would have signed the lease with you."

"You should have talked to us, Rose." Daisy, the second oldest, sounded genuinely upset. "We could have had Beckett negotiate for you, he's good at that sort of thing. We could have asked Nathaniel Denby to look over the contract."

"It's fine." Rose, sweet as could be, seemed unperturbed. Her blond hair fell in soft ringlets around her face as she opened the door to the corner shop and stepped inside with Magnolia and Daisy. Whatever she'd said was lost to Aumaleigh, but not Iris's answer.

"It's not fine! How could you have spent all that money?" Iris's oval face scrunched up with genuine distress. "This is the most irresponsible thing any of us has ever done."

"Oh, it's not so bad," Verbena soothed. Her wedding ring sparkled gaily as she set a comforting hand on her sister's arm. "It's a good idea. The baking business is growing. Besides, it's Rose's money to spend."

"But with the competition snatching up our clients, it's most certainly not a good idea." Iris's voice broke. "I can't tell you how worried this makes me."

Poor Iris. Aumaleigh looped one of Button's reins around the hitching post. "What's going on? What did Rose do now?"

"She leased the storefront," Verbena answered. "We are now officially the Bluebell Bakery. All we need is a sign to hang over the door."

"My Tyler will make one for us," Magnolia volunteered, poking her head out the open doorway, blue eyes lighting up. "Aumaleigh! So glad you stopped by. What do you think? Isn't this going to be fantastic?"

"Yes, I have no doubt." Aumaleigh couldn't help going to Iris first and wrapping her in a hug. She didn't know what the girl had been through in her life, but it was easy to see the care her sisters took with her. The shadows in her eyes were plain as day. Aumaleigh held on tight, wishing she could heal whatever was hurting the girl. When she let go, it was with regret. "The Bluebell Bakery. It has a certain ring. When do you girls open for business?"

"Tyler has to fix it up for us first," Rose explained, popping outside to grab Aumaleigh by the hand and haul her in. "He has to install the display case and put up the wallpaper. Not to mention build us a kitchen in back."

"That sounds expensive." Iris stood in the doorway, uncertain and unwilling to like the place.

Aumaleigh looked around, nodding with approval. What a cute space. It had stood empty since the cobbler had left town years and years ago. The wide windows gave it a smiling look. She could see the girls working here together, their merriment filling the place like sunshine. "I like it very much. As long as you promise I get to be your first customer. I don't think I could give you my approval otherwise."

"Who else would we want for our first customer?" Daisy swept over, beaming with newlywed happiness, her molasses brown hair falling softly around her heart-shaped face. "You will always be our favorite customer, Aumaleigh."

"Yes," Magnolia agreed, bouncing over. "In fact, we love you so much, we won't ever charge you a thing. Your money won't be good here."

"How will we stay in business if you're giving away our baked goods?" Iris wanted to know. While worry darkened her periwinkle eyes, a hint of a smile flirted in the corners of her mouth. "And, anyway, you'll be married before you know it and you won't be working here. That's just like you to give away our hard earned profits."

"It's a skill of mine, what can I say?" Magnolia teased with a light laugh.

"See, it's a good thing we're getting rid of her," Rose waltzed over, looking dreamily happy. She pushed a blond lock of hair out of her eyes, grinning from ear to ear. "We'll let her be Tyler's problem. At least that will help the bottom line. Will that make you happy, Iris?"

"Not even close." Iris crossed her arms over her chest, narrowing her eyes. "I suppose we could go to the real estate office and ask Mr. Montgomery if he'll let us out of the lease."

"Oh, he won't. I made sure to talk to him about that before I signed," Rose explained merrily. "I made him promise not to let us out of the lease, no matter what. This is a done deal, Iris. I know you need time to accept it, but trust me, you are going to love this. Cross my heart."

"You're outnumbered, Iris." Aumaleigh held out her hand to draw the girl into the circle. "A new storefront is cause for a celebration. Why don't you let me bring supper over for you girls tonight? We'll make a party of it."

"Great!" Rose clapped her hands in approval. "I'll bake a cake."

While the girls started to talk over plans and dreams for the space (Calico curtains or gingham? Lace tablecloths or sensible cotton? And how much was this all going to cost?), the back of Aumaleigh's neck began to prickle. A cold feeling dug into the pit of her stomach. She didn't have to look to know who was staring at her.

She steeled her spine, feeling the pull of him like the earth holding the moon. Once, her world had revolved around him. Once, he'd been her entire reason for living.

Don't do it, she thought. *Don't turn around. Let him walk away. Let the past stay where it belongs.* She squeezed her eyes shut, waiting for what felt like an eternity before the hairs on her nape began to relax. The prickling faded. She released a pent up breath and glanced over her shoulder at the empty boardwalk.

"We have to set a budget and stay on it," Iris was saying, her voice echoing in the empty store. "That's the only way to run a successful business."

"But we've got loads and loads of money," Rose argued gently. "Tons of it."

Aumaleigh couldn't stop her feet. They took her to the open doorway. When she poked her head out just a bit and cast her gaze down the boardwalk, she saw him one block down, walking away from her. The years had not changed the impressive, mighty span of his shoulders or the straight, muscled line of his back. Although she was too far away to hear the tap of his boots on the boards, she knew by memory the rhythm of his gait. That sound came to her now, across space and time from a past she longed to forget. It returned stubbornly, reminding her of her failures and her losses and the love she could have had, if only she'd been brave enough, if only she'd thought herself worthy of it.

But she hadn't, and so she could do nothing but watch him walk away. He was supposed to have been her destiny.

"Hello again, Aumaleigh," a familiar voice called out. Nathaniel Denby tipped his hat to her, strolling by on the boardwalk with a little girl in tow. "What's going on here?"

"This is the future sight of the Bluebell Bakery." Pride filled her as she glanced at her nieces, who were still in deep discussion, talking and laughing and arguing in the way only close sisters could. "You and your niece will have to come back when it's open for business. I bet you can sweet-talk Iris out of a free cookie."

She smiled down at the little girl, whose dark blue eyes looked too old for her sweet round face. "Make sure you bring her by, Nathaniel."

"I will. Thanks." The man tipped his hat again, continuing on his way. The girl trailed behind him like a shadow, so silent her shoes made no sound as she went.

CHAPTER SIX

"Josslyn, why didn't you tell me?" Gabriel Daniels glared at his sister, so mad he was about to explode. He stomped snow off his boots before pushing his way through the front door of her little cottage, feeling like an enraged bear on a rampage. He shoved the door closed, and it slammed with a bang that echoed in the warm, dainty front room. "You knew and you didn't tell me. I just found out from one of the men in town. Do you know what that did to me?"

"You must be talking about Aumaleigh." Josslyn, his younger sister, hardly looked contrite as she swept up a tea tray sporting empty cups and dessert plates and whirled away from him. "I thought it was best not to say anything."

"*You* thought it was best?" he bellowed. He stormed after her, tromping across the woven carpet and into a tiny dining room. China rattled in the sideboard as he pounded by. "What gave you the right to decide any of this? You know what Aumaleigh was to me. You had to know what it would do to me to find out she'd never married."

"I thought you were over her. Isn't that what you told me ages ago?" Airily, Josslyn sauntered into a tidy kitchen tucked in the back of the house. She set the tray on the counter. "Didn't you tell me in no uncertain terms that I was never to mention Aumaleigh's name ever again?"

"Well..." He came to a stop in the doorway. Anger drummed

through him with a thick, demanding beat, but her question threw him. He rubbed the back of his neck, wishing he could say she was wrong. "Yes. I did say that."

"And didn't we argue over it? Didn't we disagree?" Josslyn picked the tea kettle up off the counter and shook it. Water sloshed inside so she set it on the stove. Her auburn hair shone coppery in the lamplight and so did her anger at him. "Or don't you remember what happened the last time I begged you to talk to Aumaleigh one last time before leaving town? Or have you conveniently forgotten that too?"

"No, I remember." He hung his head, staring at a knot in the floorboards, clenching and unclenching his jaw. He felt so angry. He wanted to pound something, he wanted to stomp and storm and get out all his rage, but all he could do was sigh. "It just came as a shock to me, hearing about how she was alone all this time. She must have really meant it when she refused to marry me."

"Are you really that thickheaded?" Josslyn scowled at him. "She never married. At all. What does that tell you? All these years she never moved on. That's what you did to her."

"Me? She was the one who did the heart breaking." He had the scars to prove it. "But I know I came down hard on you back then. You were only trying to mend things between me and Aumaleigh, but they were things that could not be fixed. I was too harsh. I'm sorry. I've been sorry for over thirty years."

"I know. Me, too. Things between us were never the same after that." Josslyn's voice dipped with regret, but she was one to hold her ground. Stubbornness (and in truth, short sightedness) was a Daniels family trait. "So much so that you and I have hardly spoken in all these years."

"That's my fault. I take full responsibility." Contrite, he leaned back against the door frame and crossed his arms over his chest. He'd been a mess back when Aumaleigh McPhee had broken his heart--and boy, how she'd broken it! Shattered it into a billion pieces when she'd handed him back his ring. Apparently he still wasn't over it, because learning about her life the way he had today, unexpected and unprepared, had ripped his heart to pieces again.

Not because he loved her. No, he was over her. But because he hated what she'd done to him. Intellectually, he may have come to peace with the way they'd ended things, but apparently his heart remembered. Aumaleigh McPhee was what was wrong with women in this world. Thank goodness he'd met Victoria when he had. She'd been the sweetest lady in existence. She never would have ripped his heart out. She never would have hurt him the way Aumaleigh did.

He gritted his teeth, clenching them until they hurt. Well, perhaps he wasn't as at peace with things as he'd thought.

"The water's rumbling a little." Josslyn's practical tone interrupted his thoughts. "I'll make you a nice cup of tea. That should calm you down. Since you still seem to have your sweet tooth, I have cupcakes. Now, go sit down in the parlor and stop irritating me."

He shook his head, catching the veiled teasing in her tone. He grimaced at her. "I'll do it, only so long as you stop irritating me."

"I make no guarantees." She winked, opening a pink bakery box and hauling out a delicious looking cupcake. "It's good to have you around again, Gabriel."

"I feel the same," he confessed. He'd missed his sister all these years. The occasional letter had once felt like too much contact, back when he'd been furious at her. But that was over now. None of them were getting any younger, and one thing Victoria's death had taught him was that you never know how much time you have left. He'd come to mend fences and for two of his three children to meet their aunt and cousin.

"Besides," he added. "It's not like I'll see her again. We're leaving in a week."

"And good riddance." Josslyn winked, but tears filled her eyes so he wasn't fooled.

He felt that way, too.

* * *

Alone in her little house, Penelope tried to go about her late afternoon chores as if nothing had happened--not one thing. Certainly not that kiss, she thought resolutely, determined to pretend that her lips weren't still tingling with the after effects. The problem was, her heart hadn't beat normally since that moment when she'd been in his arms.

His surprisingly strong arms, she mused as she set a pot of soup to warm on the stove. She plunked down the lid on the pot, her thoughts drifting to that instant when she'd surrendered to his kiss. Oh, and his chest had been rock hard, too. She frowned, crossing the little kitchen to haul a loaf of bread out of the pantry. Her hand lingered on the loaf, inhaling its yeasty goodness, remembering how Nathaniel had acted after that superlative kiss.

Guess I was caught up in the moment, he'd said. *I'm sorry for kissing you.*

She frowned. Because that's what a girl wanted to hear after receiving the best kiss of her life. Sure, it hurt, but it wasn't the end of the world. It wasn't as if she was ready for romance. She wasn't in any shape to risk her heart again. No, it was still too soon after Alexander. She couldn't imagine trusting a man enough to commit her life to him and to hand over her heart. Even a man as special as Nathaniel Denby.

But it surprised her that she felt so much for him. How could that be? She set the tail end of what remained of the loaf on the cutting board (she needed to go shopping) and reached for a knife. She frowned, trying to make sense of it. Love was different for men, at least that's what she'd been able to observe. For some men--like Verbena's Zane, Daisy's Beckett, Magnolia's Tyler and Rose's Seth--they loved with all they had. They committed heart and soul.

But there was another kind of man, which was much more common. So common, they seemed to be a dime a dozen. Men who calculated and weighed and planned. Men who saw romance as a way to get whatever it was they wanted from a woman. Alexander had done it so smoothly and naturally, she hadn't even realized his true motives. He'd pretended to be ardent and devoted, but he'd had his eye on her father's company all along. A company Father wanted to hand down to his own flesh and blood--not stepsons. And since he only had daughters, that would mean handing it down to his first-born's husband.

At least Nathaniel had been honest with her. He'd apologized for that kiss immediately. He'd confessed he hadn't truly meant it. He'd been concerned for her feelings, her reputation and her comfort level in seeing him again. That firmly put him in a different category than Alexander.

Nathaniel would have been just the kind of man she would have wanted--if she'd been looking.

What she couldn't explain was why her chest felt tight. Why she was hurt when he'd only been honest with her. She didn't want a romance with him--did she? Certainly not logically, but down deep at heart something had changed. She couldn't deny it.

That troubled her all through the evening and into the night.

SWEET FOREVER

She had a hard time drifting off and when she did, her dreams were troubled. She woke up to a gray dawn where clouds hid the face of the sun, making the day dark and gloomy. She couldn't seem to lift her spirits as she went about her morning chores. Since it was Saturday, she also had errands to run and groceries to buy.

Gunderson's Mercantile was packed. Apparently many folks had the same idea to stock up on food after the storm. She wedged her way through the door, grabbed a basket and went straight for the bread display.

"Miss Shalvis? Is that you?" a rather superior voice called out above the din inside the store.

Penelope stopped in the middle of reaching for a bread loaf and blinked at the black-haired woman scowling at her. She recognized her instantly and grimaced inwardly. It was a mother of four of her students--a rather difficult mother. She put on her most pleasant smile. "Why, hello, Mrs. Crabtree. How are you today?"

"Outraged, that's what. I just sent off a missive to our superintendent." Maude Crabtree hiked up her pointy chin, perhaps unaware she had a single wiry hair sticking out of it. "I was walking home from checking on my sister-in-law when I saw the most shameful display."

Uh oh, Penelope thought, remembering she had been just down the street from Mrs. Crabtree's house. And not just standing there, either, but kissing Nathaniel. Dread filled her, icing her veins. If someone had to witness that moment of weakness, why did it have to be Mrs. Crabtree?

"I apologize," she said quickly, honestly meaning it. "I don't know what happened, it was just one of those things. I promise you it won't happen again."

"But there were children playing on the street just yards away. Children!" Maude emphasized. "Most indecent. They should not be exposed to that kind of shameful display. I expected more from you, Miss Shalvis."

"I know." While that kiss had been phenomenal, she should have had the presence of mind to remember her morals clause and the fact that perhaps those high snow drifts hadn't hidden her from view completely. "Again, I'm sorry."

"Sorry isn't enough." Maude's mouth narrowed into a straight, uncompromising line. Her dark eyes gleamed with indignation, but it was easy to see she was a very unhappy woman by nature.

Penelope felt sorry for that, even as she dreaded what was going to happen. Would Mrs. Crabtree complain? It was just one kiss. Was that a big deal? She swallowed hard, trying to control her emotions. She loved her students. She didn't want to jeopardize her job. As Maude Crabtree flounced off, Penelope stood there in front of the display piled high with bread, wondering if there was anything she could do to make things right.

"She seemed pretty mad." A deep voice rumbled behind her, a voice she knew well. Nathaniel. His chiseled, handsome face looked strained as he approached. "Let me guess why."

"You wouldn't be wrong." She grabbed a loaf of bread and moved closer to him. She lowered her voice so no one would overhear. "I don't want any problems with my job, and Mrs. Crabtree seemed pretty upset."

"She's perpetually upset." His gaze turned kinder behind the glass lenses of his spectacles. "I wouldn't worry about it just yet. I'll talk to her and see if I can't reassure her it won't happen again."

"Right. Of course." She blushed, staring hard at the loaf of bread she'd slipped into her basket. "That's a good thing. Thank you, Nathaniel."

"My pleasure." He towered over her, aware of the crush of shoppers around him, and yet it was only her he saw--her sweetness, her embarrassment and the worry tight in her beautiful hazel eyes. "It's the least I can do considering I am the cause. I was the perpetrator of the crime."

"Yes, you are. Shame on you." Mischief played at the lush curve of her mouth. "I was a helpless victim."

"Not the way I remember it, but it would be ungentlemanly to mention it." He rolled his eyes toward the ceiling, not able to believe he'd said that. "I don't want you to worry about your job. I can smooth things over. I excel at apologizing."

"You do seem practiced at it." She arched a slim, dark brow at him. "Perhaps it's because you are prone to making a lot of mistakes?"

"Gee, I wish I could say no." His gaze slid to her lips. The memory had tortured him through the night. He'd barely slept a wink. On one hand, he felt mortified at what he'd impulsively done and on the other, he wanted to do it again. He could not deny his tender feelings for the beautiful schoolteacher.

But he wasn't the only man who was interested in her. This he knew for sure. Out of the corner of his eye, he saw Lawrence Latimer angling through the crowd, coming closer. His bowler hat was balanced on the top of his head as he clutched his shopping basket with white-knuckled intensity. Likely the little man was trying to get up the nerve to talk to beautiful Penelope.

And he wasn't alone. Nathaniel glanced around the crowded store. Zeke Owens stood at the front counter, pulling greenbacks from his billfold to pay for his groceries, but his attention was fastened firmly on the town's schoolteacher. He had a faraway look in his eyes as Gemma handed him his change. He didn't look at it or count it, just shoved it in his pocket without blinking, gazing at Penelope's loveliness.

Behind him in line, Silas Meeks was busy brushing dirt off his coat and straightening his collar. Perhaps gussying himself up a bit. His gaze remained on Penelope, too, and the glint of interest in his eyes said it all.

Nathaniel frowned. Penelope clearly had three admirers, and that was only within eyeshot. How many others were out there? His stomach went tight, because this is where the pretty lady always dismissed him, turning her attention to more attractive and rugged cowboy types. But he thought of yesterday and how he'd been the one to walk away from her. He wished he'd told her how he really felt.

"I'll talk to Mrs. Crabtree right now," he promised, spotting the malcontented woman heading toward the door. "Can I drop by your home this afternoon and tell you how it went?"

"You can try, but I'll be out visiting the McPhee sisters. It's our weekly get-together." Penelope focused on him as if he were the only man in the store. "Why don't you come talk to me on Monday after school, if it's not too much trouble? I don't want to have you work today. It's the weekend. You need your family time with Evie."

"True, but I'm not working. This isn't business." He backed away, drinking in the sight of her, standing there in a light blue wool coat and matching bonnet. The straw brim framed her oval face to perfection. Little brown ringlet curls tumbled down on either side of her face, framing it, emphasizing the delicate cut of her cheekbone and her dear little chin.

Immeasurable tenderness rose up, uncontrollable and unbidden. It simply burst into life, filling his chest so fast and far there was no end to it and no beginning. He waited, hesitating for a moment for the meaning of his words to sink in and for her to gently but firmly inform him that, of course, this was business. What other kind of relationship would they possibly have?

But she didn't. A smile touched her lips--those very lips he'd kissed. He crossed the store, whipping open the door, filled with hope. Even if nothing more developed between them, he would remember their kiss for the rest of his days.

He got as far as the boardwalk before remembering something was missing. He'd forgotten to make sure Evie was behind him when he left the store. In a panic, he pivoted on his heels only to find her standing there. With her head down and her hands clenched together in front of her, she looked like a child who was used to people walking off and leaving her behind.

"That won't happen again. I promise." He knelt down in front of her, but she wouldn't meet his gaze.

She didn't believe him.

"I'm not used to being an uncle, but I'll get used to it. I'll be the best one you've ever had." He rose up to his full height and held out his hand.

She didn't take it. Skeptically, she trailed behind him on the boardwalk as he went in search of Mrs. Crabtree. The woman's horse and sled were tied up at the hitching post, so she couldn't be far.

* * *

Penelope couldn't stop the sick feeling of dread gripping her stomach. It followed her home. As she unpacked her groceries, putting everything away on the tidy pantry shelves, she thought of Nathaniel. His words intrigued her. *This isn't business,* he'd said. His low, lilting tone, the slight upturn in one corner of his mouth and his smoky gaze made her wonder. Did that mean helping her was personal? Her pulse skipped a few beats at the possibility.

Maybe she'd been wrong about his feelings for her. Hmm. Curiosity ribboned through her as she locked her kitchen door and climbed into her cutter. The small sleigh glided nearly weightless on the snow as her sweet mare pulled her through town and past Nathaniel Denby's upstairs office. The blinds were down and the windows dark. Of course he wasn't there, not on a Saturday. She bit her bottom lip, wondering how things had gone with Mrs. Crabtree. What if it went terribly and the woman carried out her threat?

She'd lose her job, that's what. What would she do? Where would she go? It wasn't as if she had family or a trust fund to fall back on. And if she did lose her job, then she would have to move somewhere else in search of work. As she nosed her spotted mare out of town toward McPhee Mansion, she remembered arriving here back in September. Bluebell had seemed like a strange, rustic place with a main street a few blocks long and a one room schoolhouse.

That first night spent in bed at her rental cottage had been a tearful one. She'd missed her sister. She'd missed her friends. She'd listened to the odd night sounds of the wilderness--the *who, who* of owls, the eerie, distant calls of coyote, the rustle of raccoons in the yard outside, and even, once, the growl of a bear strolling by. How hard it had been for a city girl to try to sleep with all that going on! She shook her head at herself, chuckling. But the sturdy walls had kept the wildlife out and come morning, she witnessed the most beautiful dawn ever. Soft peach and gold streaks lit up the eastern horizon where earth and sky met.

Montana Territory's beauty had captured her and she never tired of it. Autumn had been a spectacular show of vibrant leaves in all shades of oranges, reds and yellows lighting up the surrounding hillsides and mountains. Winter had come with its frosty snows, disguising the landscape and making it fresh and new. The mountains gleamed white at the sun's touch, but on overcast days like this, it felt as if the peaks themselves were sleeping, simply waiting to wake.

McPhee Mansion came into sight between snow-laden trees. The elaborate estate reminded her of the gingerbread houses she and her mother used to make when she was small. She spotted another horse and vehicle at the hitching post and reined her darling mare, Alice, alongside the sleigh.

"Hey, stranger!" Verbena McPhee Reed looked up from fastening a wool blanket onto her new mare, Poppy (which her new husband had bought for her). Verbena was a striking beauty and even more so now that she was happily married. "I'm so glad you could make it. Iris made her fabulous split pea soup for lunch, and I'm guessing she whipped up some of her buttermilk biscuits to go with it. It's so good, you could die from it. It's the only thing that could drag me away from my Zane."

Merriment sparkled in Verbena's sapphire blue eyes as she grabbed her knitting basket from the back of her new sleigh. Luminous and joyful, Verbena was excellent proof that true love was out there. A girl just had to find it.

Penelope frowned. Why did the image of Nathaniel Denby enter her mind?

"What is Zane going to do without you for a few hours?" Penelope asked, hopping out of her sleigh. "He must be lost. No idea what to do with himself."

"Oh, he's been invited over to the sheriff's house. He and Milo are old friends." Verbena trudged through the deep snow, looking dear with her hat tied around her chin and her brown curls bouncing. "He'll be just fine. Besides, it won't hurt for him to be around Milo's girls. One day he's going to be a father."

"Oh!" Penelope's heart leaped with hope as she shook out Alice's warm horse blanket. "Do you mean--? Are you--?"

"No, not yet. But it's inevitable." Verbena blushed sweetly. "I think Zane will make a wonderful father."

"Me, too." Penelope hefted the blanket over Alice's back. "I would pay good money to see that rough and tough former bounty hunter of yours holding a baby."

"Me, too." Verbena laughed. "I can't wait. What about you?"

"Work has been wonderful, although the Dunbar boys keep me on my toes." She did her best not to think of Nathaniel and his kiss. Or the fact that he might be speaking to Mrs. Crabtree on her behalf right now. "Those boys can be so funny. Some days it takes all my might not to let myself laugh at them. The last thing they need is encouragement. Just think, maybe one day you will have sons and I will get to teach them."

"Boys?" Verbena shook her head, hooking the basket handle around her arm. "I can't imagine boys. I grew up with sisters. What would I do with boys?"

"Toss them out with the bath water," she teased. "You don't have to keep them."

"Funny, but wait--" Verbena's eyes filled with emotion. "I'm imagining little Zanes running around my house. Oh, I think I'm going to cry."

"Okay, then you should definitely keep any boy babies." Penelope knelt, groping beneath her mare's belly, trying to find the blanket's buckles.

"Miss Shalvis, let me get that for you," a man's voice broke in politely. His uneven footsteps came to a stop behind her.

"Why, Oscar. Thank you." She smiled at the man the McPhee sisters had hired to help around their house. "That's very nice of you."

"It's no problem, Miss." Oscar was in his thirties with light brown hair and a pronounced limp. He approached her cautiously, the gentleman that he was, although clearly down on his luck. His clothes, while clean and pressed, had seen better days. He worked for the McPhee sisters now. "I'll make sure your mare is good and snug. You just go on in and get warm. Howdy, Miss Verbena."

"It's just Verbena. And, Oscar, it's a pleasure to have the sidewalk shoveled. Look at that. It's a much better job than I ever did."

Oscar blushed humbly and buckled the blanket.

"Although you have Zane now to shovel your walkway," Penelope pointed out, fetching her reticule and crochet basket from the floor of her cutter.

"Yes, I do have Zane." Verbena went back to smiling broadly again. "Lucky me."

They hurried down the walkway together. Verbena's happiness was contagious. The gray day felt brighter as Penelope breezed along. If only she could stop worrying about Mrs. Crabtree. Her stomach was in knots.

"So," Verbena said cryptically. "What else is new with you? Maybe it has to do with a certain man in town?"

Penelope's foot missed the bottom porch step. Her jaw dropped in surprise. She gasped for air. "What does that mean? What did you see?"

"Oh, I heard a little gossip is all," Verbena said innocently, but the front door swung open, and Iris McPhee stood in the grand foyer in a lovely blue dress.

"I was just beginning to worry about both of you." Iris, the oldest McPhee sister, took her worrying seriously. She was a quiet beauty with strawberry blond hair and periwinkle blue eyes. "Did you have any problems on the road?"

"It was just slow going," Penelope explained, forcing her feet up the steps. Her chest felt fluttery, the way it did when something was wrong. What gossip had Verbena heard? And what if more people, aside from

Mrs. Crabtree, had witnessed that kiss? A cold panic spilled into her bloodstream, making her shiver.

"Come in and get warm," Iris urged, holding open the door. "Once you thaw out, Penelope, you'll have to tell us all about you and Nathaniel. I heard all about your big kiss."

"You did?" Her shoulders slumped. She crossed over the threshold, the panic in her blood kicking up a notch. "How did you know? Has Mrs. Crabtree been talking?"

"Our aunt witnessed it first hand," Rose called out from the kitchen, her voice echoing merrily down the long hallway. "Aumaleigh told us all about it. It was long and passionate and so sweet, it made her sigh."

"Oh, Penelope." Verbena shrugged out of her coat. "This is truly wonderful news. I don't know why you're keeping it to yourself, but we're your friends. Tell us everything."

"There's nothing to tell." She set her basket and reticule on the nearby entry table. "Nathaniel just needed to talk to me about his niece."

"We heard about the niece, poor thing," Iris sympathized, her love for children evident as she gave a sad sigh. "It just breaks my heart."

"Mine, too," Penelope agreed, tugging off her gloves, relieved at the change of subject. "She's just a little dear. She's lucky to be with Nathaniel. I'm sure he'll take good care of her."

"Yes, Nathaniel." Rose poked her head around the doorway to waggle her brows. Apparently the subject hadn't changed at all. "Now, what about that kiss?"

"It was an accident." Penelope held up her hands helplessly. For all she knew, Nathaniel still hadn't meant that kiss, and she didn't want to make the mistake of saying otherwise--although she was hopeful. A little thrill zinged through her, a little piece of happiness speeding through her entire being.

"How can a kiss be an accident?" Verbena wanted to know, taking Penelope's coat from her and hanging it up on the coat tree. "Did you stumble and fall and your mouth landed on his?"

"Yes, that's exactly what happened," Penelope teased, and everyone laughed. "Nathaniel apologized and now everyone thinks he's beauing me."

"We think it because it's true or it's about to be." Rose waggled her brows again. "Come on back. I'll pour the tea while we wait for

Magnolia."

"Is Daisy coming?" Penelope asked, heading off down the hallway, finally hoping the topic of Nathaniel's kiss was over and done with.

"After she fixes lunch for her handsome husband and their beautiful daughter." Rose whirled around, her skirt twirling behind her as she tapped into the kitchen. She wasn't alone. Elise Hutchinson stood at the counter, stirring a pot of split pea soup.

"Hi, Penelope," Elise greeted warmly, looking lovely in her fashionable, tailored wool dress. Her dark hair was down, tied simply at her nape with a velvet ribbon. She was the hallmark of country gentility--lovely, kind and a good friend. "What's this I hear about you and Nathaniel?"

"Inaccurate gossip," she teased. "Don't believe it."

"Right. I won't give it another thought," Elise teased back knowingly.

The front door banged open on a gust of wind. Cold air coursed through the house, and Penelope shivered.

"Shut that door!" Iris called with a tray in hand. "You're letting out all the heat."

"Sorry. The wind is picking up." Magnolia hollered back. "It was a long drive, but I got the cake delivered on time. It's going to be so much easier when we work out of the shop in town. Brilliant idea, Rose."

"I know," Rose said happily, grabbing an oven mitt and rescuing a sheet of perfectly golden biscuits from the oven. "It's just the start of my plans."

"Somebody stop her quick." Iris rolled her eyes at the ceiling. "Verbena, get the bowls. Elise, give me that ladle, you're a guest, and guests should not be doing the cooking. Rose, what happened to the tea?"

"It's on the table," Rose said cheerily. Magnolia strolled in, full of good cheer, and the back door swung open to reveal new bride Daisy, rushing in as if she feared she was late. Laughter and conversation filled the kitchen, and Penelope gave Nathaniel one last intriguing thought before she joined the sisters.

CHAPTER SEVEN

"Well, her front door window is lit. That's a good sign. Penelope must be home." Nathaniel glanced over his shoulder before crossing the residential street. Tiny snowflakes fell lazily, so delicate they looked like bits of lace waltzing down from the sky. They sailed beneath his hat brim and caught on his eyelashes. He blinked, stealing a look at his niece, who traipsed along silently behind him.

If Evie was glad Penelope was home, she gave no sign of it. She walked safely an arm's length from him, hands buried in her coat pockets, teeth chattering. He'd asked her again to put on her new clothes (much warmer clothes), but she shook her head adamantly.

Dusk was falling, casting long shadows down Penelope's shoveled walkway and onto her small front porch. He stomped snow off his boots, trying to pretend his heart wasn't pounding. He ground his teeth, wishing he didn't like Penelope so much.

You're going to get hurt, man. He didn't see any way around it, not really, but he rapped his knuckles on her door. He had to see this through.

Muffled footsteps tapped closer on the other side of the wall. His throat went dry. His palms went damp. He fought the urge to run and save his heart while he could. Evie waited on the steps behind him, faithfully keeping her distance.

This could go wrong, he thought woefully. *Very, very wrong.*

The curtain on the window next to the door swept back, revealing Penelope's lovely face. Her hair was down, tumbling around her face and falling over her shoulders like liquid molasses. The lamplight burnished it, turning it to shades of rich auburn and deep copper. Recognition traveled across her face and she flashed him a smile that made every brain cell in his head forget to function.

If only he was more experienced around women, he thought ruefully as Penelope disappeared and the curtain fell into place. But he'd never been much of a dandy. He'd never had a way with the ladies. He pushed his glasses higher up on his nose and swallowed hard when he heard the bolt turn. The door opened. Penelope stood in the fall of lamplight wearing her winter coat, lovelier than the last time he'd set eyes on her. She was lovelier every time he saw her.

"Nathaniel, what did I tell you?" She frowned at him with her soft mouth, with those lips he'd kissed so tenderly--and wanted to kiss again.

"It's nearly suppertime. Surely this could have waited until Monday unless--" Distress etched across her face, making her look even more dear. "Unless things went terribly with Mrs. Crabtree?"

"Actually, no. They went better than expected." Nervous, he took off his Stetson and shook the snow from it. Not a brilliant move because now the falling snow landed on his head. Flecks of white clung to his eyebrows.

Not exactly the most dashing thing.

"Whew. What a relief." She huffed out a sigh of relief. Her hand flew to her throat. She squinted into the dark. "Evie, is that you? I can hardly see you standing all the way out there."

Evie shrugged one shoulder in answer but didn't move. Nathaniel ached for the child, but he figured Penelope was right. Evie needed time to adjust and to learn that she could trust him. It wasn't easy, but he would give her that time. He'd do anything he could for her.

"I hope you don't mind that we came by tonight. Evie didn't want you to worry a moment longer than necessary," he explained, plopping his hat back on his head. "Neither did I."

"All right, so, give me the news. Wait. I have a question first." Penelope wrapped her arms around her middle, troubled. "Will you represent me when the superintendent comes to talk with me?"

"Sorry, I won't." His baritone dipped, warm and soothing. "Because I talked to Mrs. Crabtree. She isn't going to complain to the superintendent."

"Really? You did that?" Oh, she couldn't believe it. It was too good to be true. She rocked back a few steps, overcome. "You mean she's not mad anymore?"

"Not when I explained it was all my fault. You know it was." He leaned one shoulder against the doorframe, peering down at her with kindness--she'd never seen anyone so handsome. He cleared his throat as a blush crept across his face. "I just reached over and kissed you before you had a chance to stop me. You were taken by surprise."

"At first I was, yes." She had to be honest. She also had to be honest about the pain tightening behind her sternum like a closing fist. Why did it hurt to hear how he hadn't meant that kiss--when she already knew? She tried to swallow, but her Adam's apple wouldn't move. "But for honesty's sake, I didn't push you away like I should have."

"That's right. You could have pushed me away. You could have had a fit. You could have put me in my place." He seemed happy about that. Manly lines bracketed his mouth. Hints of dimples dug into his lean cheeks. "But you didn't. I apologized to you for that kiss, but I didn't mean the apology. Not at all."

"You didn't?" Her head snapped up.

"Nope. But I did mean every moment of that kiss." He strode across the threshold so they were face to face. "Just so you know."

Speechless, she met his gaze--his honest, guileless gaze. This was how it felt when a man told you the truth, she realized, seeing the strength of Nathaniel's sincerity, of his heart.

Her heart responded against her will--even though she was not ready to trust another man so soon. Feeling flooded her chest--soft and sweet, tender and true.

"Were you going somewhere?" he asked. "You're wearing your coat."

"No, I just got in. Right this moment. I haven't even taken off my coat or lit the fire yet." She felt flustered, her stomach all a flutter, her head a little dizzy. So, Nathaniel had meant that kiss, had he? She hid a smile, shrugging out of her wraps. That was interesting news--good news, she decided. She liked him very much.

"Here, let me help." His fingers grazed the underside of her chin. The sensitive skin there exploded with sensation--the sweetest thing she'd ever known.

"Thank you." She slipped her arms from her coat, aware of his nearness. She'd never felt like this before--part elation and part comfort. Was this the way it should be between a man and a woman? She was woefully inexperienced in the matter. When she'd been with Alexander, she'd mostly been on pins and needles, always trying to make things work between them.

"It's freezing in here. Let me light the fire for you," he offered, striding farther into the parlor. "Evie? Come on in, sweetheart."

The child on the doorstep wandered in and closed the door behind her. Evie stood just out of reach of the lamplight, clinging to the shadows. Head down, she stood there with her hands clenched together and didn't move.

Furrows dug into Nathaniel's forehead. Clearly he was concerned. She was, too. This wasn't the child she'd seen at school or playing with Sadie Gray. Sure, Evie had been withdrawn then too, but this was different. It was as if the child had vanished completely, and she was simply a form standing against the wall, as if she'd pulled so far into herself there was nothing left.

Nathaniel was right, she realized. He did need help with this child, far more than she'd imagined. Something was terribly wrong. She couldn't imagine how much Evie might be hurting. As she led the way deeper into the pitch black, unlit parlor, she reached for the lamp next to the sofa, but stubbed her toe on something hard instead.

The little table it was supposed to be resting on rolled around and into the reach of the single entry lamp. She blinked, not able to make sense of it at first.

"What happened here?" Nathaniel's voice boomed. He whisked the lamp off the table by the front door and carried it into the parlor.

It was a shambles. Tables and cushions were on the floor, her carpet was missing. She glanced over her shoulder to peer into the kitchen and saw that her coffeepot was gone. Her stomach twisted. "I've been robbed."

"Robbed?" Nathaniel sounded as shocked as she felt. "There have been minor things at the businesses in town, but not this. Look at your kitchen, Penelope. They went through all the drawers and your pantry."

"My groceries." She circled around the table in the center of the room, staring at the empty shelves she'd just stocked this morning. What was going on? Why had someone done this?

"The back door has been kicked in." Nathaniel disappeared into the dark corner. Strength boomed in his voice. "I'll go fetch the sheriff, but I don't want to leave you here alone. Let me take you next door."

"I don't think I should go. This is my home." Cold tremors began to seize her. Shock was setting in. Her knees shook hard, so she backed up and leaned against the wall for support. She'd gone icy from head to toe. "I'll wait here."

"No, you won't." Nathaniel's boots pounded against the floor, knelling with a strong, uncompromising rhythm. "What if they come back? You would be here alone with them. No, please trust me. Let me take care of you."

His voice dipped, rich and kind. Her heart responded like a new flame feeding on air. Was it wrong that she'd always wanted a man to speak to her that way, to look at her with great affection in his eyes? He took her by the hand--his big, strong hand--and guided her around the debris. He blew out the lamp, leaving it on the counter and held the door open for her.

"Come on, Evie," he said. His gentleness toward the child only made her adore him more.

Don't get ahead of yourself, Penelope, she thought, easing down the shadowy steps. A low moon peered over the trees, tossing a gleaming platinum path along the snow. It felt like a fairytale to walk along the darkly glittering snow with her hand enfolded with his. Nathaniel stayed protectively at her side, shielding her from the wind, his strength more reassuring than anything she'd ever known.

If I'm not careful, she thought, *I'm going to fall so fast and hard in love with him there will be no escape.* She squared her shoulders, fighting to hold onto her heart.

Nathaniel knocked on her neighbor's kitchen door. It swung wide to reveal a smiling blond woman whose apron covered the first telltale bump of pregnancy.

"Penelope? Nathaniel?" Maebry Blackburn gave a soft laugh. "I'm not surprised at all to see you together. Don't think I didn't spot you two walking off side by side after the blizzard. Come in, come in. Gil, be a love and put the kettle on the stove for me? Lucky I baked cookies today. Come sit by the fire and I'll get some--"

"This isn't a social call." Nathaniel cleared his throat. He didn't want to put a damper on the young couple's happy evening, but it had to be done. "Penelope's house was robbed, when she was away this afternoon. Can she stay here while I run to fetch the sheriff?"

"How awful!" Maebry's face fell. "Of course she can stay. Gil, we were home all afternoon. Did you see anything?"

"Not a thing." The tall, strapping assistant foreman for the Rocking M ranch moseyed over. "Why don't I go with you?"

Nathaniel nodded his agreement, ready to head back out the door. That's when he spotted a certain fragile shadow hovering outside on the back step in the cold. Evie shivered, staring hard at an icicle hanging off the overhead eaves. Why hadn't she followed them inside? He wanted to haul her into his arms and hold her tight until that dejected slump to her shoulders disappeared, but he knew she'd only run if he tried. His chest ached with frustration and helplessness. "Can my niece stay here with you ladies?"

"Absolutely." Maebry squinted out into the darkness. Apparently she'd heard the rumor about his niece's arrival to town, too. "Hi, there. I hope you like chocolate cookies. I sweet talked Iris McPhee into giving me her recipe, but I had to swear on my honor I would keep it a secret forever and ever. That's how good the cookies are. Would you like to try one?"

Evie gave a slow, single nod.

"Then come sit by me, sweetie," Penelope invited, pulling out one of the ladder-back chairs at the round oak kitchen table. Her warmth toward the child mattered. A lot. Affection tangled up in his chest for the woman, and it wasn't easy fighting it down.

"Let's go." Gil grabbed his coat from the wall hook and shrugged into it, stepping out into the night with pure determination.

That's how Nathaniel felt, too. He wanted to protect Penelope and make sure she was safe. He tipped his hat to the ladies and headed outside. As he grabbed the knob and pulled the door closed, he caught sight of Penelope. She watched him through her long, thick lashes, and his chest kicked hard. He could tell himself a thousand times not to hand over his heart, that love never worked out for him. He couldn't help it. Penelope Shalvis was worth the risk.

* * *

Sheriff Milo Gray sprinkled a little more flour into the pan and stirred. The gravy was peppery and greasy, just the way he liked it, and it was just about the right thickness too. Heat from the stove radiated across his face as he tilted his head to one side, realizing there was silence. His girls weren't squabbling. Sadie wasn't trying to jump off the top of the banister and kill herself. Sally hadn't stabbed herself with her play princess sword.

A real moment of peace. That was a rare thing in his life. He gave the gravy another stir. His mother was always after him to find a wife. She always said that would help matters if he didn't have to cook all the time, not to mention it would mean there would be a motherly eye on the girls at all times. But marriage wasn't something he took lightly, and honestly, it wasn't easy finding an eligible lady in this part of the country where marriageable females were a scarce minority--let alone finding a woman who didn't pale and run at the sight of his daughters.

"Ow!" An outraged little girl's voice shouted from the front room, shattering the silence. "Pa! Sally stabbed me again."

"It wasn't me, Pa. Honest." His youngest pitched her sweet, high voice so it was particularly adorable. "It was Mitsy. Mitsy did it."

"Mitsy can't use a sword," Sadie protested at the top of her lungs at a shockingly high volume. It was a wonder the window glass didn't rattle in its panes.

"It was her horn," Sally explained just as loudly. "It was an accident. She didn't mean it."

Mitsy was an imaginary baby dragon. Milo frowned, grabbed a towel and used it as a hot pad to lift the pan from the stove. He held it over the gravy boat, aimed and poured. "What did I tell you about Mitsy?"

"I dunno," Sally hollered back. She was good at pretending to forget things.

He rolled his eyes, set the fry pan on a trivet on the counter and hauled the gravy boat into the dining room where a roaring fire popped and crackled in the grate. "If Mitsy can't behave in the house, then she'll have to stay outside on the porch."

"But it's too cold for her on the porch." Concern drove Sally's pitch even higher and she came running, rounding the corner with wholehearted worry. "She could *freeze*, Pa. She's just a baby."

"Then maybe you should put her on a leash." He sometimes said things just to amuse himself. Clearly the joke didn't go over well. Sally frowned.

"She's not a dog." Her sweet little face dropped. Even her wooden sword sagged toward the floor. "She's a dragon. A *dragon*, Pa. Those are extremely rare."

"It doesn't matter." He didn't dare let his weakness show. He had a great big soft spot for his girls, and if they knew it, then he'd never keep the upper hand. All would be lost. So he turned on his heels and moseyed back into the kitchen. "You tell Mitsy if she can't behave, then I'll have to lay down the law. Now, supper is ready. Go get your sister and come eat."

"What if Mitsy pokes her with her horn again?" Sally asked angelically.

"Maybe you'd better leave your sword and Mitsy here with me," he suggested, grabbing the platter of sliced roast and the bowl of whipped potatoes. "Go on, hurry or the food will get cold."

"All right, but be sure and watch her, Pa." Sally admonished. She was going to grow up to be a schoolmarm with that tone. She dropped her sword with a *clunk* on the floor and dashed off.

Milo sighed. Maybe he could hope for a few more moments of peace? Maybe even a quiet meal without an argument, accusations or a food fight? It might be too much to wish for, but a man had to have dreams.

"Stop pushing!" Sally hollered, pattering into the dining room. "Pa, she's pushing me."

"I'm not pushing her. I'm shoving her." Sadie grinned at him saucily as she followed her sister and circled the table.

"And she was touching me, too," Sally reported as she hauled out her chair.

"Do I need to arrest her and toss her in jail?" Milo asked, setting the meat and potatoes on the table. "I can cuff her right now. Make her spend the night in a cell."

"Sally touched me first," Sadie informed him, plunking down in her chair. She looked a little ragged with her straight blond hair tousled and windblown. She'd run wild today in the streets, tobogganing and snowball fighting and who knows what else. Truth be told, he didn't want to know. It was easier on his heart that way. It was under enough stress as it was.

"Guess you'll both be spending the night in a cell." He grabbed the back of Sally's chair and pushed her in before taking his place at the table. "That sounds all right with me. I'll have the place to myself. Lots of peace and quiet. I can catch up on my reading. Eat up all the dessert your grandma sent over."

"Grandma made us dessert?" Sally perked up.

"What'd she make us?" Sadie demanded, grabbing her fork. "Maybe it's chocolate cupcakes. I told her we'd really, really like some."

"You'll never find out, because you aren't getting any." Milo grabbed the meat platter and doled out slices onto the girls' plates. "You'll be locked up, remember? I get those cupcakes all to myself."

"Pa, you wouldn't do that to us." Sadie grinned at him, a pretty little thing even in the boy's shirt and trousers she wore. She was going to be a heartbreaker one day. "It's because you love us."

"Yeah, and you can't lock us up because Mitsy will get lonely." Sally smiled sweetly up at him.

"I suppose I can let you girls off easy this time." He sunk a serving spoon into the mound of mashed potatoes and scooped some onto Sally's plate. "But next time, I'll show no mercy."

A loud, no-nonsense rap on the front door echoed through the house. Milo grimaced, returned the spoon to the bowl of mashed potatoes and pushed back his chair. "You girls stay right here and eat. Got it?"

"Yep," Sadie said around a mouthful of potatoes.

Sally stuck her finger into the gravy boat and nodded.

Frowning, Milo rose from his chair and crossed the room. He didn't have to wonder who was on the other side of that door. It was about work. He had no doubt. No one came knocking this time on a weekend evening if they didn't need the sheriff. He grabbed his holster off the top shelf on his way to the door and buckled it on. When he yanked open the door, two familiar men stared in at him from the dark, lightly speckled with snow.

"Milo." Nathaniel Denby nodded in greeting, his jaw tight and his stance tensed. Something was really wrong. "We got a problem."

Milo had a bad feeling. It was the same feeling he'd had when Ernest Craddock had come to town--a hollow in the pit of his stomach, a prickle at the back of his neck, the sense that things were about to get a whole lot worse before they got any better.

CHAPTER EIGHT

Penelope tried to ignore the sick, shaky feeling vibrating through her. She took a sip of the mellow, lavender chamomile tea that Maebry had brewed, but the sweet warmth couldn't begin to soothe her. It was as if the heat from the stove couldn't reach her. All she could think about were her possessions littered across the floor. A stranger had gone through her things. She swallowed hard against a rising lump in her throat.

You'll never make it on your own, Father had pronounced in his no-nonsense, the-world-will-bend-to-my-will way. *A woman like you is too weak to survive in this world. Men will prey on you. You don't know what villains are out there, my dear. I've protected you from it all, and you're too foolish to know it. You'll fail, mark my words. There will come a day you will wish you did what I wanted.*

Down deep, she was afraid he was right. She stared miserably into her cup, trying to push those words from her mind. But they stuck stubbornly, refusing to budge.

This isn't failure, she thought, straightening her spine. It's just one of those things that happen in life.

"Oh, she's breaking my heart." Maebry's whispered comment caught Penelope's attention. She blinked, looked up and followed Maebry's gaze.

Evie had retreated to the stove, stubbornly staying in the kitchen, nibbling slowly on the cookie Maebry had given her.

"Such tiny little bites." Maebry's blue eyes filled with tears she swiped away. "She must be trying to make the cookie last. I can't take it anymore. I'm giving her a second one. I'll be right back."

Before Penelope could answer, Maebry pushed out of the overstuffed chair by the gray stone hearth and rushed into the neighboring room. Penelope knew just how she felt. She kept wondering, too. What more could she do to help Evie? She turned in her chair. The little girl stiffened as Maebry approached. The sweet woman struck up a one-sided conversation as she lifted the lid off the cookie jar.

Penelope's heart ached watching the child. If only Evie would open up and talk. Then at least Penelope could find out what was troubling the child. But how to reach out? She thought of all the books she'd left back in Boston--Father tossed her out before she could retrieve them. Some of those books had been wonderful resources on child care. She longed to go to them now and leaf through their pages seeking answers. Perhaps she could visit the bookstore in Deer Springs? But no, her gut told her the answer Evie needed could not be found in a book.

"Lights are on in your house." Maebry poked her head into the room, concern on her face and sadness in her eyes. No caring person could look upon the child and not feel sorrow for her. "If you would like to run over and talk to the sheriff, I'd be happy to keep an eye on Evie."

"Thank you, Maebry." There was no one sweeter in this town. Penelope grabbed her coat, hesitating at the sight of the girl seated on the floor in front of the cook stove. She looked so lonely sitting there. "Evie, I'm going to go talk to the sheriff. Don't worry, your uncle will be back in a few moments to fetch you."

Evie's shoulders sank further. She lowered both cookies and set them on her knee. Penelope hesitated. She wanted to fix every hurt and hug the girl until all her loneliness went away, because she knew how that felt. She'd lost a mother, too.

"Go on," Maebry urged. "I'll take care of her."

Surely, there could be no better person to leave Evie with. Penelope ducked out the door and blinked against the snow blowing into her face. It came down harder now with steady, unrelenting beats. She waded down the path and across the yard where light from her kitchen door spilled onto the back steps.

"Penelope." Nathaniel filled the doorway, the lamp at his back, but even in silhouette his strength shone through. Perhaps even more so, she reasoned, because beyond his bookish appearance and mild manner, he was mighty. Why did her heart have to beat faster at that?

"The sheriff just left. He's following the tracks the robbers left before the storm gets any worse." Nathaniel reached out, drawing her through the doorway and into his arms. It was such a wonderful feeling being tucked against his chest. Safe and secure, protected and cared for. Breathless, she gaped up at him, dizzy, not exactly sure if the ground was still beneath her feet. All she could see--all she wanted to see--was him.

Another set of footsteps knelled in the parlor behind her.

"Miss Shalvis." Deputy Wade Wetherby stalked closer, his notebook and pencil in hand. "We need to determine what the robbers took."

"Robbers, as in two of them?" She stepped forward, grateful that Nathaniel's hands came to rest on her shoulders. He stood behind her, a presence, a man she could count on.

"Milo said so, judging by the tracks. They didn't bother covering their trail out back," Wade explained, tipping back his Stetson. "With any luck, those tracks will lead Milo right to them. Now, can you look around and tell me what's missing?"

"The parlor carpet, for one thing." She was not happy about that. It had been an indulgence, spending far too much of her budget on it, but it had been soft and warm for her feet this winter. She bit the inside of her cheek, wrestling down a strange stab of pure anger. "A lamp is gone. Let's see. They took my coffeepot. The kitchen is such a mess, I can't tell what's missing. I'll need to sort through it."

"Obviously someone is redecorating," Nathaniel quipped, although his eyes shone fierce. "They took what they could carry. It bothers me that they must have done this with people nearby. We need to question the other neighbors, Wade. Just because Gil and Maebry didn't see anything doesn't mean others didn't."

"I agree." Wade's jaw tightened as he looked around. "Miss Shalvis, can you write up a list? I can come by in the morning for it."

"Of course." She pushed a brunette tendril out of her eyes, lifting her chin. Her hands shook a little, but her stance was steady. "It's only possessions, just stuff. I'm thankful I wasn't home at the time, and that no one was hurt."

"Me too, Miss." Wade tipped his hat, taking a moment to study the elegant schoolteacher up and down.

Nathaniel couldn't blame him, but he didn't like it either. He held the door open for the deputy. "Thanks for coming, Wade."

"Sure thing." Wade straightened his shoulders, puffing out his chest. Wade was a good-looking man, powerful and charismatic, the kind who always hooked a lady's attention. He shot Penelope a dashing grin. "Looking forward to seeing you tomorrow, Miss Penelope. Trust me when I say I'll do my best to catch those varmints. They did wrong to pick on a lovely lady like you."

"I appreciate it so much, Deputy." Penelope gave a polite nod but nothing more--not one thing more--as she waved him on his way and turned to gaze around her mess of a house, planting her hands on her lean hips. "Well, Nathaniel, this has been quite an exciting evening."

"Probably not the kind of evening you were hoping for." He gave the broken back door a push, gauging the damage to the hinges. Minor and easily fixable. "So much for a quiet night at home, huh?"

"Who needs quiet anyway?" She spun with a swirl of blue and when she looked at him, soft emotions darkened the copper threads in her beautiful eyes.

Was that admiration he saw? Was that attraction? His heart swelled, and he shuffled his feet, staring down at the toes of his boots to gain his composure. He had no words for how much that meant.

"Surely you need to get home." Penelope padded toward him, stepping over cooking utensils scattered across the floor. "You only meant to drop by and tell me about Mrs. Crabtree."

"Oh, I don't mind staying." He turned his attention to the hinges because there was so much he felt in his heart that he didn't know how to say. "Cleaning up is going to be a big job for just one person. Don't they say the load is lighter when more people carry it?"

"That's true." She knelt to the floor, gathering up spatulas and serving spoons. Her skirt belled around her and the lamplight graced her, polishing her with a soft golden glow. She kept getting more beautiful to him every single day.

He suspected that's the way it would always be, that she would be more lovely in his eyes as time went by. It was as if he felt the ground shift, as if life would never be the same from this moment forward. That was fine by him.

SWEET FOREVER

* * *

Penelope smoothed her duvet cover back into place and fluffed her remaining feather pillows. Her bedroom was nearly in order. She looked around with satisfaction, trying to forget the fact that some strange man had been in this most private of rooms and had touched her things. She'd already picked up her undergarments from the floor and tucked them into the laundry bag. No way did she intend to wear them until they'd been washed. Honestly. She'd be lucky if she could ever wear them again.

"Do you need anything repaired in here?" Nathaniel hesitated in the doorway. He blushed slightly, staring down at the floor, such a gentleman.

She adored him for that. "No, they did no damage in here. They searched through my bureau for valuables, but what little jewelry I have is at the bank. It's odd what they helped themselves to."

"I find it odd too." Nathaniel backed into the parlor as she strolled toward him, making room for her. He looked grim, his forehead furrowed with concern. "They cleaned out your pantry. They took a rug, a lamp and a fry pan."

"At least they left the tea." She picked up her notepad and scribbled down *two feather pillows* on her list of stolen items. "But they took the coffee. Oh, and my stack of dishtowels is missing. Do you think it's a homeless person? Or someone down on their luck stealing for his family?"

"That's one way to look at it, a very positive way." Nathaniel set the hammer he held down and considered the polished oak end table laying on its side. "You look for the good side of things, don't you?"

"I've always been a glass-is-half-full kind of girl." She glanced down at her list. A few forks, spoons and knives were missing. Her coffeepot. Her coffee mill. "It's like someone is taking what they need for a home. Do you think it's one of the poor families here in town? We have some desperately poor families."

"The Redmonds come to mind." Nathaniel considered the possibility. "Clint Redmond lost his job at the mill when he fell so ill with scarlet fever."

"I heard he nearly died, that it was touch-and-go for a long while." Penelope hated to think of how one illness could tear a family apart. She adored the four little Redmond children--two girls and two boys.

Such sweet kids.

"Yes. His wife and another child passed." Nathaniel lifted the end table and set it into place beside the sofa, his tone full of sorrow. "It was a sad thing. His health didn't come back fully, and he's been out of work. He might be desperate enough to take only what he needed for his children, so I could see someone like him taking some food, but not this. A decent man would never leave a mess like this."

"So, what are you telling me?" She swept a fallen doily from the floor and set it neatly on the top of the end table. She was a little afraid of the answer.

"Sometimes we have outlaws just passing through town and they steal what they need. They are desperate men too, but cut from a different cloth." Nathaniel planted his hands on his hips, studying the room. "Those men are dangerous. I don't like to think people like that were in your home."

"Me, either." She gulped, trying not to give in to her fear or to the sound of her father's voice in her head. "That's why I'm staying on the positive side. Do you think they will come back?"

"I want to say no. At least, that's what I hope." Nathaniel walked over to her favorite reading chair sprawled on its side and righted it. He tucked the cushions into place. "That's why I put in a stronger latch on both doors. They won't be getting in easily if they try again."

"Oh, I hadn't noticed. Nathaniel." Her hand flew to her chest, touched by his thoughtfulness. "Where did you get the latches? I should reimburse you."

"When I borrowed Gil's toolbox, I asked him to run to the hardware store." He simply shrugged as if it were no big deal, as if he helped women in distress every day. "The owner lives above the store. He'll bill the landlord."

"I still should reimburse you for all you've done. You've spent part of your Saturday afternoon--wait." She glanced at the little mantel clock lying on its side on the floor, still ticking. "It's after seven o'clock? We've been at this for hours."

"Time passes when you're with good company, I guess." His voice dipped low, full of meaning.

She nearly dropped the clock, wondering if he was talking about her. "Oh, I'm not good company. It must be you."

"Me? Not possible. I'm boring, or so I've been told." He gave a self-conscious shrug and righted the overturned ottoman. "The most exciting thing I do is read."

"Me, too!" She exclaimed, gathering up the little decorative throw pillows she'd made long ago for her hope chest. She tucked them neatly against the back cushions of the sofa. "Right now I'm reading Jane Austen. How about you?"

"Charles Dickens." He knelt in front of the fireplace to add some wood into the grate. "It's how I spend a lot of my spare time. I don't think Evie knows what to make of me sitting in my chair staring at a book for hours on end. I've offered to read to her, but she doesn't want me to. It might be my imagination, but she looks at me as if I'm strange."

"I used to get those looks from my family all the time." She took a step back to inspect the room. While it was once again in order, it wasn't as cozy without the carpet. Not to mention a little dark with only one lamp. "My stepbrothers would make fun of me, my stepmother feared I would never marry if I kept reading like that. She said it wasn't attractive to a prospective husband, but I didn't care. I wouldn't want that kind of husband anyway."

"I like a woman who reads. But that's my personal opinion."

"Why, thank you for understanding. My ma was a reader." She gave a little sigh, remembering her dear mother. Her quiet nature was bruised by Father's harsh and controlling ways. "She used to read to me when I was very small. I loved it so much, she would eke out pennies from the food budget to buy me books of my own."

"She sounds like a kind woman." Nathaniel reached for the little fireplace broom and swept the bits of bark into the hearth. "I bet she was every bit as kind as you are."

"Oh, Nathaniel." She placed a hand over her heart, not sure why this man had a direct route to it. His words mattered very much. "I think her books were a refuge from my father's treatment of her. I know they were for me."

"That's what they were for me after my mother died." He put the broom away slowly, his jaw working as if he was debating the merits of saying more. "It was a difficult time, missing her so much. It seemed like nothing would ever be good again. Pa buried himself in a bottle and never came out. The whiskey turned him into a different man, someone who had no concern for his children. Books were a comfort to me then, and now they've become a way of life."

"A wonderful way of life." She ran her fingers across the few titles sitting on the corner shelf. The books had been toppled over but not knocked to the ground. Likely the thieves saw no value in them. She straightened them, volume by volume. "I couldn't bring many with me, but that's okay. I'm building a new collection. As for Evie, I'm sure she doesn't look at you strangely. You really aren't all that strange."

"Thanks. I appreciate that." He thumbed his spectacles higher on his nose, his dark blue eyes alight. "I'm sorry you had a controlling father. That had to be difficult to grow up with."

"He caused immeasurable heartache, especially to my mother. It was hard to watch as a small girl, seeing how he took pleasure in hurting her and in, well, owning her. He saw her as his possession." She winced at the note of hurt she heard in her own voice. She'd never been so honest with anyone about this before. "Ma made me promise that when I married someone, it wouldn't be a man like my father. She said there are good men out there, like the kind in my books. I made a vow of honor to her that I would wait for a man like that to marry."

"So that's another reason why you had to break off your engagement." Nathaniel paced closer, crossing the shadowed floor, seeming to bring the light with him. "You owed it to your mother to do the right thing for your life."

"Yes." Her breath caught as he came to a stop in front of her. She wanted him to kiss her again. She wanted to be swept up into his arms and held against the hard span of his chest, whether it was wise or not.

"I, for one, am very glad you decided to become a teacher and move here." He tucked the strand of hair behind her ear, his touch amazingly gentle. His fingertips brushed the outer shell of her ear and she trembled, quaking all the way down to her toes.

"Me, too," she whispered, her face heating. She glanced down, staring at the middle button of his blue flannel shirt. Her heart felt too open, as if he could look inside and read her feelings and see… everything. Everything she was afraid to hope for.

As if he felt the same way, he leaned closer. His eyes went black, shining with tenderness, and his gaze traced her mouth. He wanted to kiss her. Yes, this was everything she hoped for. Heart pounding, she tilted her face up, breathless as he slanted his lips over hers. First contact was gentle and light, sweet and respectful. A soft caress of his lips to hers before he pulled back.

It wasn't enough. She bit her bottom lip in protest, to keep the words unspoken. She wanted more. The emotion in his eyes shone so gently she felt as if she were basking in light. He covered her mouth with his again and kissed her completely. *Really* kissed her, until her toes curled and her entire body melted.

Nothing, ever, was more perfect than that kiss, and she never wanted it to stop. Her hands landed on his arms. Her fingers curled into the fabric of his sleeves, holding on. When he breathed, she did too. For that one moment, their hearts beat in synchrony, in perfect rhythm. It was the sweetest thing she'd ever known and the most thrilling. When he pulled away, they were both smiling.

"I thought you promised Mrs. Crabtree that would never happen again." She let her eyes twinkle at him with mischief.

"Well, I promised her I would never kiss you in public." He brushed away a tendril of her rich, brown hair out of her eyes. "And look around, it's just the two of us. No one can see us. As you can see, I'm a man of my word."

"Yes, you are." She blushed. "I like a man who keeps his promises."

"Good because keeping promises is the thing I do the best." He blushed. Well, it's getting late. It would be proper for me to go."

"Uh, yes. I suppose so." She could hardly concentrate. She felt balanced on the edge of a high precipice, and she was falling. A little thrill of fear charged through her, followed by a bolt of joy. "I do have that morality clause."

"No male guests in your home past seven o'clock." He gestured toward the mantel clock still sitting sideways on the floor. Neither of them moved to retrieve it. "It's thirty-two minutes past the hour."

"How do you know the exact clause?" she asked him.

"I drew up the contract for the superintendent. There are just two schools in the entire district." He didn't move a muscle, but he felt closer somehow, as if no distance separated them. "That's two violations for you in two days."

"It's because of you. You're a bad influence." She meant the words playfully, but they didn't come out that way. The moment between them felt too solemn, too rare.

"Me, a bad influence? I suppose there's a first time for everything." He winked, as he backed across the room, leaving her standing there staring at him with her heart on her sleeve. She couldn't hide her feelings.

She didn't want to.

"Good night, Miss Shalvis." He stopped in the entryway and pulled his coat off the wall peg. "If Mrs. Crabtree is out there noticing I'm here so late, maybe peering out her window to see what you're up to, you just let me know. I'll calm her down."

"You do have a surprising way with women." Penelope didn't have to think--her feet were already carrying her toward him. "I need to be careful around you. You're one of those lady's men. A real charmer."

"That's me. I have a handful of women all dangling on a string." He winked, shrugged into his coat and reached for his hat. Merriment curved his mouth upward, softening the lean lines of his square face. "I've never been the serious type."

"Right." She didn't believe that for a second. She'd never met anyone more sincere. "Thanks for everything, Nathaniel. I feel bad that I pulled you away from a nice evening with Evie."

"Being here with you was my pleasure. Do you feel safe staying here alone for the night?" The merriment faded from his gaze. Concern replaced it. "You could spend the night somewhere else, with one of your friends maybe? I would be happy to drive you wherever you want to go."

"That's a nice offer, but I'll be fine." She raised her chin, fisting her hands, determined. "Have a very good night, Nathaniel."

"You, too, Penelope." He smiled when he said her name. He stood in front of the door in the little vestibule for one long moment. His gaze turned black and intriguing as he studied her. In that silent moment, she wondered if he was thinking about kissing her again. But she would never know because he turned away, reached for the door and stepped out into the night. "Good night."

"Good night." Her lips tingled as if disappointed there was no kiss. She hung her head, a little ashamed of herself for wanting a second kiss from him so soon. Alexander had waited until he'd slipped a ring on her finger before venturing to kiss her in his wet, slippery way.

Now that she had been kissed by Nathaniel, she understood what a kiss should be. It was just as it was in books. She pressed her fingertips to her mouth, tingling with the memory of that kiss--that wonderful, magnificent kiss. She was never going to forget it for as long as she lived.

Long after she'd closed the door, she stayed standing in the chilly foyer, unable to move. Going over every moment of the evening--how he'd come with good news, how he'd rushed her next door so she would be safe while he went for the sheriff, how he'd repaired every broken hinge and helped her return her little cottage to its usual, tidy state.

And as much as he'd done, it wasn't the things he did that got to her the most. It was the emotional support she'd felt. He cared. He worried. He wanted to make sure everything was all right for her. It felt so good to be treated like that, tears burned behind her eyes. She mattered to him--she did, just her. Not for any other reason or any other gain. He'd done this for her because he cared.

Her heart lit more brightly, burning in a way it never had before. She went to the kitchen, listening to her shoes knell on the hardwood and echo against the walls. Her house felt so lonely without him. Feeling vulnerable, she filled the tea kettle and set it on the stove. Tea would comfort her. She needed it after the robbery.

Strangers had violated her sense of sanctuary. They'd handled and taken her things. But it didn't feel random. It felt personal. The dark shadows in the corners of the kitchen, just beyond reach of the light, felt blacker tonight. She felt smaller.

Her father's words came back to her. *A woman like you is too weak to survive in this world. Men will prey on you. You don't know what villains are out there, my dear.*

In a way, down deep, she still feared he was right.

The kettle began rumbling on the stove and she reached down a stoneware cup from its shelf. It was a comfort what Nathaniel had said. He was right--whoever had broken in here was desperate. But they'd chosen an empty house to steal from and they hadn't harmed anyone physically. They'd taken only things--things that could be easily replaced.

She reached for her teapot and measured tea leaves, feeling better now, feeling stronger. A light knock rapped on her front door. By the time she'd crossed the parlor and turned the knob, the knocker was long gone, but a wicker basket was sitting on her door step. Dinner, by the smell of it.

Goodness, what a surprise. She uncovered a loaf of bread, a crock of delicious smelling bean soup and a bowl of fresh eggs (for breakfast come morning). There was no note, but she didn't need one. She could feel him out there in the dark. She would know his presence anywhere. Caring filled her, and she lifted a hand in thanks to Nathaniel Denby, wherever he was, out there in the dark. She grabbed the basket's handle and stepped into the warmth of her home.

She really was falling for that man. Really, really falling. But was it wise, could she trust him with her heart? That was the question. She used the new latch and carried the basket into the kitchen, feeling joyful at the possibility.

CHAPTER NINE

Nathaniel waited until after Penelope had retrieved the basket of food, closed the door and locked it before he headed next door. The image of her standing there in the light, staring out into the dark with a soft smile stuck with him--and so did that kiss. He liked taking care of her. His chest swelled with tenderness so great it hurt.

If this doesn't work out, I'm going to get hurt. Big time. That thought accompanied him as he trudged through the snow and up the shoveled steps. He swiped hard falling snow out of his eyes, wishing there was a way he could protect himself, but love wasn't like that. You had to jump in with both feet, come what may. He just wished he had more experience with a serious relationship. He wished he was better at speaking his feelings.

The front door swung open and Maebry stood there, pulling on a heavy wool shawl and waggling her brows at him. "What are you doing here? You were supposed to stay there and eat with her. You know, have a little romantic meal together."

"Penelope's had a long day." He shrugged, making excuses, he knew, but she'd had a hard thing happen with the robbery. He didn't want to take advantage of that and try romancing her when she was vulnerable. "This is better for her."

"I suppose." Maebry shook her head at him, scattering her soft blond curls, her Irish brogue like a melody as she wagged a finger at him. "How am I going to get you two together if you keep thwarting me? It only makes me want to try harder."

"While I appreciate the help, I have plans." But he was perfectly capable of courting a lady on his own. "If I need advice, I'll come knocking. Thanks for watching Evie tonight."

"It was my pleasure. She's such a good little girl. She ate every bit of her supper." Maebry's tone dipped low as she held out her hand to the girl out of his view and pulled her into the doorway. "Evie has got her coat on and she's ready to go. Evie, thanks for keeping me company tonight. Goodbye, sweetheart."

Evie nodded twice, giving Maebry a shy smile before tumbling across the threshold and onto the porch beside him. She sidestepped to a safe distance and waited patiently, staring hard at her shoes. She seemed to withdraw again. This was twice now he'd noticed her less protected and withdrawn with other people. But when it came to him, she tucked herself up like a turtle in its shell. She wouldn't even look at him.

He couldn't say that didn't hurt. It troubled him as he tipped his hat to Maebry and led the way off the porch. Evie trailed behind him like a distant shadow, barely making a noise. Frustration built inside him, but more than that, it was a worry that he might fail. He didn't know what to say to the girl to help her. He didn't know how to express his affection for her.

Truth be told, he didn't know how to talk about affection to a woman either. But surely Penelope knew how he felt. Their kisses had been proof enough, right? He stopped by the sheriff's house on the way home to find out if the thieves had been caught, but Milo's mother answered the door. He hadn't returned home yet. Sadie came to the door and chattered away to Evie, who nodded and smiled and waved an emphatic goodbye.

He was half-frozen by the time he arrived home. He stomped snow off his boots as he climbed the front steps, pulled out his key ring and shouldered open the door. Evie stayed on the porch until he'd tugged off his boots, lit a lamp and had retreated farther into the front room. He could hear her teeth chattering as she closed the door and bent to wrestle off her snow-caked shoes. He could see the ice on her socks from the holes in them from all the way across the room.

It frustrated him. Why didn't she wear her new shoes? Apparently she didn't seem to want anything from him. Nor did she want to be near him. As he uncovered the embers in the belly of the stove and fed them moss and kindling waiting for the fire to grow, he wondered if it would always be like this. What if she never took to him? He hated to think of it, but would she be happier with someone else? Maybe there was a woman relative out there who would take her, someone Evie would rather be with.

He straightened up slowly, surprised at how much that thought hurt. He was taken aback by how much he cared for little, lost Evie. And then he knew why. She was the spitting image of his baby sister with that sloping nose and tiny curve of a chin and that long straight hair so fine it was always escaping its braids. He loved her. It was just that simple.

All she needs is love, Penelope had said. Well, he had that. It had to be a start. Encouraged, he lit another lamp and broke the silence. "Evie, do you know what your mother used to like?"

He waited a beat, hearing the slight rustle as the girl shook her head.

"She liked it when our ma read a story to us. Now I know you shook your head no the last time I offered, but I happen to have your ma's favorite story on my bookshelf." He tried to keep his voice casual, but he didn't feel casual. Not at all. Too much was at stake. He could not fail at this. He lit the match and touched the flame to the lamp's wick. "I haven't read that book in a long time, and I've been wanting to read it again. Would that be okay?"

No answer. At least she hadn't shaken her head *no.* Nathaniel blew out the match, wondering if he'd just made some progress. He sure hoped so. He lowered the glass chimney onto the lamp base, skirted the end table and sofa and circled to the bookcases lining the wall. It took a few moments to find the book he had in mind. The instant his fingers touched the well-worn binding, soft and slightly tattered with age, it all came back. The laughter before Ma's death, the hot summer days playing in dandelion-studded fields and when it was too hot to play, settling down on the shady porch with Ma to listen to her read to them. His little sister would sprawl out on her stomach, chin propped on the heels of her hands, feet crossed in the air.

When he glanced at Evie, he was reminded again of the resemblance to his sister, and what she would want him to do for her daughter.

"Come on over." He lowered his voice, gesturing toward the sofa as he eased into his overstuffed chair. "Get comfortable because this is a good story. Your ma would always plead with our ma not to stop reading it. It's that good."

Evie's eyebrows shot up with interest and she unclasped her hands, rocked forward and rushed out from the shadowy entryway. Her toe caught on of the end table and her momentum sent it sprawling. The lamp clattered to the floor, the glass shattering. The table hit hard, echoing like a gunshot. The lit wick licked at the edge of the area rug and caught.

Evie stood frozen still, horror carved across her round face. The fire was inches away from her. Nathaniel tossed down the book, lunged from the chair, pulled her away from the small flame and rolled the carpet over on itself until there was nothing but smoke. Adrenaline spiked through him as he turned around, looking for anything else on fire, but the floor wasn't even scorched. Sharp shards of glass glittered, but none of them had cut Evie.

The girl had retreated to the far wall by the window. Her back was to him, her spine curved into a C as she slumped into herself, her hands to her face. Her regret and fear were so palpable, it hovered in the air.

"Evie?" He ventured toward her carefully. He didn't want to scare her. "Everything's all right. The fire's out. It just got the very corner of the rug. Why don't you come sit down while I sweep up the glass?"

A single, racking sob broke, shaking the frail little girl hard.

That shattered his heart. He took a few more steps toward her, but she stiffened up like a board, wincing as if expecting a hard, hard blow. He stopped, aghast. Someone had beaten this child. Badly. Rage licked in his gut and he fisted his hands, not knowing what to do. Penelope had said love would fix this, and he was truly grateful for her advice right now. More than anything.

He tamped down his own anger, set it aside and focused on Evie. If he were her, what would he need? He knew what it was like to be a child and afraid. He remembered the frightening man his father had become as a drunk. He took a slow, deep breath and knelt down alongside the girl. She braced herself again, but he didn't let that stop him. From this moment on, nothing could. He'd do his best to say what he felt.

"I don't know what it was like for you living with your other uncle, but things are very different here." He laid the flat of his hand on her little back, feeling the hard slash of her rod bones and the knobs of her vertebrae through her clothes.

She gasped, too terrified to move away.

That didn't stop him. He rubbed soothing circles on her back, the way his ma used to when he'd been sick as a boy. "That was an accident. Accidents happen sometimes. It's okay. When you're ready, why don't you go over and sit on the sofa for me. I'm going to clean up the glass, fetch another lamp and we'll start reading."

She held in another sob with a hiccupping sound. He couldn't see her face, still buried in her hands. Her body felt so tense, he didn't think he had made any kind of a difference at all. At a loss, he climbed to his feet and retreated into the kitchen to grab another lamp, the broom and dustpan. Evie still hadn't moved a muscle when he returned to the room. She stood hunched and braced, waiting for a punishment that would never come.

Well, she'd figure that out soon enough. He wrapped his fingers around the wooden handle, swept up the glass, picked up the metal kerosene well which was still full and hadn't punctured (thankfully). He hauled the carpet through the back door and left it to air out on the porch. On his way back to the front room, he stopped to pour milk into a pan and set it on the stove.

"I think this calls for hot chocolate," he said gently, peeking around the corner. "I have enough for two big cups."

Evie parted two fingers and stared at him with one eye, perhaps to check his sincerity. He settled into his chair, opened the book and began to read. It took twenty minutes before she ventured out from her place by the wall, and by then, he'd already rescued the hot chocolate from the stove and brought in two big cups. She settled silently into the far corner of the sofa, studying him over the rim of her cup.

She was looking at him. Finally.

With a smile, Nathaniel continued reading.

* * *

A mile out of town on the slope of a forested hillside, two brothers hiked out of the cover of the trees, pulling a hand sled in their wake. The cabin in front of them stood like a drunken sailor leaning against a post, sagging at the spine. It wasn't much, but it was home--Pa's home. He'd let them live here.

Junior dropped one of the sled's ropes, hiked to the slumped front door and pushed it open. He remembered Christmas spent at the jail with Pa. It was still all he could think about. They'd shared a turkey dinner. Pa had looked at him with such hope, as if Junior were actually important to him. Pa was counting on him. Remembering put a swell of pride in his chest.

"It's coming down hard enough now." Giddy, his younger brother stopped on the step to look back. "That stupid sheriff won't have a chance of finding us."

"He won't, no matter what. I covered our tracks good." Junior grabbed the lantern sitting inside the doorway and struck a match, protecting the flame from the hard wind with his body. The wick flared, tossing dancing light across the dirty floorboards and the weathered walls. "Don't just stand there. Start unloading. I got me a hankering for a nice cup of coffee."

"Too bad that uppity schoolteacher didn't have whiskey in her pantry." Giddy unwound the rope securing the load and grabbed a stuffed burlap sack off the sled. "I told ya, we should've hit the mercantile. They had whiskey."

"You can buy whiskey, stupid." Junior marched out into the storm and yanked the burlap sack from his brother's hands. "I found ten whole dollars in her underwear drawer."

"We're gonna eat good tonight." Giddy lifted a second sack from the sled and inhaled it. "Hmm. Ham. We're gonna eat like kings."

"It's what we deserve. The way it ought to be." Junior grabbed the second sack from Giddy and carried both through the snow and into the frigid cabin. He looked around at the squalid little place. It wasn't much. Just one room, with two bunk beds built into the back wall, a stone fireplace and rickety furniture. Not at all like that teacher's house.

Fury raged through him. Why did a woman live better than they did? Every second he'd been going through that house, his bitterness had grown. Pa had worked his fingers to the bone, slaving away for a decade for that McPhee family, and what did he have to show for it? Nothing but a jail sentence. That family had gotten rich off his father's hard work, off the backs of the folks that worked for them. And the schoolteacher was friends with the McPhees. It didn't bother him one whit that he'd taken from her. She could afford it. Besides, she got what she deserved.

And so would he.

"I like this lamp. It's gonna give off lots of light." Giddy stomped in, leaving snow everywhere. He set the fancy glass lamp on the table on his way by. "Think how warm our feet are gonna be with the rug."

"It's just the start." Giddy promised, reaching inside one of the bags to search for the coffeepot. He'd get the stove going and the coffee boiling and then he'd head out for the last bag of goods.

Thanks to the schoolteacher, they had enough food to last the rest of the month, not to mention a few comforts. The rug was a nice touch. Maybe they didn't have to live so poor, not anymore. He considered that, bending down to stir the ashes. Maybe they didn't have to wait until they had it all to be comfortable. They'd take what they wanted along the way, until they'd made the McPhees pay for everything that family had done to Pa.

Every little thing.

* * *

Morning had finally come. Penelope yawned, left the cook stove door open to feed the growing flames and crossed the kitchen. The wind battering the north side of the house held a watery note. The snow had turned to a rain mix sometime around three in the morning. She knew because she'd been awake. Every small creak of the house or gust of wind snapped her wide awake, which was pointless because last night's vandals were not coming back in this weather.

She yawned again and pulled back the pink calico curtains. The chunky mix of snow and rain pummeled the window pane, smearing it, making it hard to see out. The dark gray morning dripped with gloom. Wind whipped snow from the trees in the backyard and water poured in rivulets off the eaves. She shivered in the chilly damp and really missed her coffeepot. Nothing warmed you up on a winter morning like a nice steaming cup of coffee.

A knock on her back door echoed through the room, bouncing off the walls. It couldn't be Nathaniel. Just the thought of him made her smile from ear to ear and head to toe. She dashed to the door and whipped it opened.

"I heard what happened." It was Josslyn Daniels who pushed her way in out of the inclement weather. "Well, I saw the sheriff come over last night and leave following tracks. Don't think I'm not nosy enough to sneak over and ask Maebry what happened. She promised

Nathaniel she'd make sure you had coffee this morning, but I said I'd do it. Maebry's still under the weather with morning sickness."

"Thank you, Josslyn." Wonderful. She could hug the woman. Coffee. Leave it to Nathaniel to think of that. "Will you stay for a bit and have coffee with me?"

"Oh, I would love to stay and gossip." Josslyn rolled her eyes toward the ceiling, considering it. A curl tumbled down from her knit hat, curling delicately against her face. Time had taken its toll on that face, but pleasantly so. Josslyn, even in her fifties, had a touch of real beauty. "Maybe just one cup. You look like you didn't sleep, my dear. You were brave staying in this house by yourself."

"Not brave, more like stubborn." She fetched two ironware mugs from their shelf and plopped them onto the counter. "Besides, the thieves were likely family men down on their luck. They chose an empty house to break into. I don't think there was ever any real danger to me."

"You are too soft-hearted." Josslyn grabbed the jug, uncapped it and filled two cups. "But you're young yet. I used to see the good in folks, but then I wised up."

"Is that right?" Penelope took a sip from her cup. "You really don't see good in people anymore?"

"No, I try and see the bad. That way I know what I'm dealing with." Humor dug lines around Josslyn's expressive eyes as she studied Penelope over her cup's rim. "I like to be prepared. Forewarned is forearmed. We've had a lot of trouble with vagabonds and outlaws wandering through, taking what they want from folks instead of working for it themselves. It boils my oil, I tell you. The nonsense that Ernest put the girls through, obsessed with Verbena the way he was. Pathetic. The girl didn't want you, man, move on with your life. But no, he had to follow her here and kidnap her. We're lucky he didn't do worse. No, I like thinking about the bad in people."

Penelope bit her bottom lip to keep from chuckling. Josslyn was a riot. "What about me? You must see the bad in me, too."

"It's terrible the way all the children in town love you. Parents sing your praises. It makes me suspicious, it does." Josslyn winked before taking another sip, stalking over to the little table and pulling out one of the chairs. She settled down as if she owned the place. "What's this I hear about you and Nathaniel? I have it on good authority that he stayed to help you clean up last night."

"That's true. I can't deny it. He's a gentleman." Her face heated as she pulled out a chair. Her lips buzzed with the memory. Would she ever forget that kiss? She plopped down onto the cushion and rolled her eyes. Probably not. That kiss was indelibly etched into her brain for good.

"Oh, I saw him kiss you, remember? I saw it with my own two eyes." Josslyn leaned back in her chair, giving a soft trill of laughter, deeply amused. "Tell me, will wedding bells be ringing for the two of you before long?"

She nearly choked on her coffee. She swallowed, coughing a little and set down the cup. Honestly, she and Nathaniel weren't even beauing. "I have no immediate plans, especially since I tend to be unlucky in love."

"There's always an exception to every rule. Not that I've ever been lucky in love, mind you." Josslyn raised her coffee cup in a salute. "But I have a good feeling about you and Nathaniel. I--"

A knock on the door interrupted. Mulling that over, Penelope rocked to her feet, deciding that she had a good feeling about her and Nathaniel, too. Bad luck streaks were made to be broken, right? Her heart beat triple time thinking about the way he'd taken care of her last night and even had thought to have someone look after her this morning, when it wouldn't be proper for a gentleman to be seen at her home. Especially with nosy Mrs. Crabtree living a block away.

She opened the door to a spray of lumpy rain and stared out at the unfamiliar but handsome man on her back doorstep. He was a well-preserved man in middle life, with dark hair and charcoal gray eyes.

"I followed my sister's tracks here," he explained, tipping his black Stetson. "Josslyn, you invited us over for breakfast, remember?"

"Oh, I didn't think you were coming." Mischief flashed in Josslyn's eyes as she rose from the table. "I thought you were mad at me. I figured you probably never wanted to visit again, the way you did last time when you were angry with me."

"I know, I'm wrong." He raised his wide shoulders in a resigned shrug. "But I've learned a few things since. For instance, it's wise to never let an apology stand in the way of a good meal."

"Men. With logic like that, it's no wonder you are all lost without us." Josslyn winked on her way by, drawing her scarf tightly around her neck. "Don't forget what I said, Penelope. Sometimes something great comes into a woman's life. If she doesn't grab on tight with both hands, it'll past her by, never to come around again. Believe me, I know. Now, you have a good day. Don't let the rain get you down."

"I won't. You have a great day, too." Penelope held the door open as Josslyn passed through, feeling buoyed by the older woman's words. "Thanks for bringing over the coffee."

"It was my pleasure, dear." Josslyn led the way down the steps and into the deep mess of wet and melting snow. Her brother gave a polite tip of his hat before heading off in his sister's wake.

Penelope closed the door, thoughtful. She wandered over to the stove. After Alexander had humiliated her and broken her heart, she'd been afraid to hope real love could happen for her. She was old by Boston standards, a spinster that her stepmother's friends and her stepbrother's wives had *tsked* at, shaking their heads with pity. Poor Penelope, destined to be alone and unwanted. As her father liked to say, the bloom had gone off the rose. It hurt.

It still hurt.

But the funny thing was, here in Montana she didn't feel like an old, used up spinster. She felt as if her future was full of possibilities. Maybe it was because she was starting over with a new home and a new job. Maybe it was that the McPhee sisters and even Josslyn's cheer was wearing off on her, but when she'd found out the only man who'd ever courted her couldn't honestly manage to actually love her, she'd lost her confidence.

Well, maybe she wasn't ready for the shelf just yet. Maybe she still had a little bloom left. Nathaniel Denby could turn out to be the one man who could honestly love her. She reached for the bowl of eggs, which had been in Nathaniel's basket last night and reached for one of her fry pans. The memory of their second kiss blazed into her mind, making her lips tingle and making her hope.

CHAPTER TEN

Gabriel Daniels stood at his sister's front window, gazing out at the rain driving from sky to earth like a cold gray curtain. The roads were a mess out there. He could see three sleighs and sleds stuck in various parts of the street. Two of the owners had abandoned their vehicles, leaving them stuck in the slushy but still deep snow. One lone man remained, shoveling out his home-built sled with dogged determination. With every shovelful he made, the vehicle just sank deeper into the heavy snow. Poor fellow.

"Makes me glad we walked over." His nephew, Seth, a big and strapping man in his own right, ambled up with two steaming cups of coffee. He handed one over. "A smart man would stay inside today. I've enjoyed your visit here, but I'm worried about you leaving to head home."

"Me too. I'm hoping it will be easier going by then." Gabriel took a sip of the bracing coffee and winced at the scalding liquid scorching his tongue. It burned all the way down. He shrugged. "It wouldn't be the worst thing if we had to delay the trip."

"Don't you have to get back?" Seth joined him at the window.

"Well, I suppose we do. Leigh is in her final year of school. Liam has work to get back to." He blew into his cup to cool it, weighing things. His daughter had her friends and her social life (not nearly as important as school to her). His son took his job seriously but was enjoying his visit to Montana. He watched steam curl up from his coffee, considering. "I suppose if we arrive home a few days late, it won't be the end of the world."

"What about you? What about your ranch?" Seth blew on his cup too.

"I've got a foreman I can trust." His life in Ohio seemed a lifetime ago. That's because seeing Aumaleigh in town had rattled him to the core. The shock of seeing her still got to him. Here he'd thought he was over her, that he was at peace with what she'd done to him. A smart man would head back home as soon as he could. He wouldn't want to linger here where he could bump into her again. "Maybe the roads will be fine. I'll keep a positive outlook. So, why did you have to move all the way out here to the wilderness?"

"It wasn't my choice, it was Ma's." Seth grinned in his easy-going way, his mop of slightly curly dark hair tumbling over his forehead. "It's all her fault."

"I heard that!" Josslyn hollered from the next room, where kitchen sounds rose and fell--the clank of a pan, the clink of the oven door, the chime of glassware being set on the table. Josslyn pitched her voice to rise above all the noise. "It's not my fault at all. It was Maureen McPhee. She's the one who bribed the county land agent to let her homestead so many sections of land. Guess she had to come all the way out here to find a corrupt agent."

"Well, it worked out for me." Seth grinned, his dimples digging deep. He had the look of a satisfied man, a man who'd found the right woman to love for the rest of his life.

Gabriel was real glad about that, and he was glad he'd been able to help the boy out. "You got lucky with Rose. You're lucky she forgave you or you might be singing a different tune."

"I wouldn't argue with you there." Seth gazed out at the street again. "I was going to take her out for a sleigh ride this afternoon, but I'm not sure I can make it out to her house."

"Boy, I don't think you could make it if you walked there." Gabriel shook his head. The poor love-sick kid. "Stay home. One Sunday can go by without you courting her. Give the girl a rest."

"Maybe I will walk." Seth pondered the possibility.

Gabriel rolled his eyes. Yes, he'd been there too, more times than he could count, willing to do anything for a woman. It was a rare privilege to have that depth of feeling.

"Breakfast is ready!" A singsong voice rang out. His Leigh (hard to believe she was nearly all grown up) sailed into the room in a pretty pink dress with her rich brown hair down, curling everywhere. She was as pretty as a picture. He had to blink twice, trying to reconcile this grown-up daughter with the little girl he remembered, so fragile and small she used to sleep tucked in one arm, safe against his chest. She frowned at them, shoving a lock of hair behind her shoulder. "What are you two standing around for? That platter of bacon is going to be gone in two seconds. I left Liam alone with it at the table. Oh, look at that poor man stuck in the snow."

"I was just thinking of going out and helping him, now that I'm done with my coffee." Gabriel tipped the mug, draining the last drops. He was never himself until after his first cup. "Guess you'll have to save some of that bacon for me if you can."

"I could try," Leigh teased, her gray eyes sparkling, proof that she intended to do more than try. Leigh was headstrong enough to succeed at whatever she set out to do, even if it was rescuing a few strips of bacon from her brother.

"Better save some for me, too." Seth set his empty cup down on the windowsill. "The job will go quicker with both of us."

"I won't argue with that." Gabriel headed toward the entryway and pulled on his coat, not thrilled to step out in that nasty weather.

"I'll save some eggs and fried potatoes, too," Leigh called out, hurrying over to close the door after them.

The wind was mean, no doubt about it, but Gabriel followed Seth around the side of the house to dig two shovels out of the garden shed. The residential street had a lonely feel to it as Seth called out to the man, who'd stopped shoveling out his stuck sled and stood, puffing heavily, swiping sweat from his brow. Beside him, his swaybacked donkey lifted his long ears curiously.

"Hey, Lawrence." Seth ambled over amiably. "Looks like your cart is stuck."

"For the fifth time this morning." The little man with a bowler hat, narrow rounded shoulders and a handlebar mustache looked like he was fighting gloom. "I wanted to be the first to ask the lovelier than lovely schoolteacher to go on a drive this afternoon."

Gabriel shook his head, glad he was no longer a courting man. He was done with that, good and done. That was fine by him. But that didn't mean he couldn't remember what it was like to be a bachelor with courting on his mind. He shook wet snow out of his boot and took another step.

Yes, he remembered courting well. The little Ohio town he'd moved to way back when hadn't been this tiny. No, it had been a good deal bigger with streets and streets of shops and every convenience. The first time he'd set eyes on Aumaleigh had been on one of those streets. He'd simply been picking up some grain at the feed store when she'd climbed out of a buggy on the other side of the road. Once his eyes landed on her, his heart had never been the same.

"Today might not be the best day to go courting." Gabriel informed the little man as he gripped the wooden handle tight and drove the shovel deep beneath the cart's wooden runners.

"I know, but I can't waste time," the little man named Lawrence answered, hurrying over to dig in with his shovel too. "It isn't easy in a town like this. There are too many of us bachelors. I wasn't fast enough last time and broke my heart over a fair damsel."

"Fair damsel?" Gabriel arched a brow at Seth, but Seth only shrugged and went to work on the opposite side of the cart. It was hard to tell what this little man's problem was, but he seemed harmless enough.

"Yes, Seth captured the affections of one of the fairest of them all." Lawrence's mustache drooped sadly. "But I'll survive. I've had my eye on the fair Penelope for some time. I'm going to make my intentions known today."

"Is that right?" Seth kept a straight face as he continued to dig. "I heard a rumor that Nathaniel Denby is sweet on her."

"Oh, I haven't heard that rumor." Lawrence's narrow shoulders slumped dejectedly, panting heavily as he shoveled away.

Seth answered the little man, but Gabriel didn't hear it because something caught his attention down the street. A woman on horseback, oblivious to the drum of the rain, stopped in front of the corner house and dismounted.

It was her elegance that snared him, tugging at some distant memory. He recognized her straight, graceful posture as she dismounted and the slim line of her arm as she unhooked a saddlebag. Aumaleigh. His pulse stalled in his veins, his blood refusing to move. He wasn't prepared for this, he didn't want to see her in person.

Panic surged through his chest. He snapped his gaze away, but it wasn't fast enough. Against his will, he caught a glimpse of that sweep profile, her adorably sloping nose and the curve of her dear, heart-shaped face. He tipped his hat low to hide himself from her. He held his breath, waiting through those long seconds until he was sure Aumaleigh McPhee hadn't noticed him.

Seth was still talking with little Lawrence, but Gabriel couldn't make his ears hear the words. His heartbeat strained, clapping like thunder in his eardrums. He didn't like the way his hands were shaking. Why was he reacting like this, after all these years? What Aumaleigh did to him was a lifetime ago and his life was better for it--at least, that's the way he had to see it. Aumaleigh had done him a favor, rejecting him the way she had, when he'd loved her so deep and true. He'd gone on to meet Victoria, who'd been the sweetest woman alive. She'd given him three fine children and a life he wouldn't trade for anything.

But somewhere deep inside, feelings stirred. It was a place in his heart that remembered--a place he'd been sure had died when she'd shattered it.

The rain pounded against his cheek and dripped down his face. He sank the shovel into the wet snow, fighting the pull of the past. It was too strong. It sucked him under, taking him in, making him remember.

The sun scorched his back as he bounced along on the buckboard's seat, reins in hand. The leather straps were damp against his palms. How could he be even more nervous over a second date than the first? He shook his head at himself, sure he was a sorry excuse for a man.

The cowboys he worked with had given him all kinds of advice. Some had cautioned him not to show his feelings too soon. Others advised to play it cool and aloof and never give her the upper hand. Still others had told him not to go at all because courting was dangerous. It ended in marriage. But one sage old man had told him to be direct and honest. There was no greater reward in this life than the love of a good and kind woman.

That described Aumaleigh perfectly. Gabriel leaned back against the seat, smiling to himself, still a little dazed that such an incredible beauty would look at him twice, much less let him come courting. The shirt he'd ironed three times stuck to his skin as he reined his team around the corner. Anticipation beat through him as the late May wind caught the brim of his Stetson. His heart beat wild and crazy, fearing he would mess up today or say something stupid. Worse--maybe she would see he was just an average, normal fellow, nothing special at all, and change her mind about him. What--what if she already figured that out and wouldn't be waiting for him like she promised?

The buckboard swung around the corner, giving him a glimpse of the wooden rail fence and Aumaleigh McPhee in a butter yellow dress. Her molasses-dark hair was down today, tumbling over her slender shoulders. The ribbon of her hat caught the wind, brushing the curve of her beautiful face.

Tenderness overtook him, so bold and bright it drown out his very substantial fear. In that moment, a soul-deep stillness settled in. Peace filled him from head to toe. He could see his future so clearly. Aumaleigh's smile. Aumaleigh's hand in his. Aumaleigh walking down the church aisle in a wedding dress, destined to be his wife.

His entire life spread out before him--tender nights, happy days, her body rounding with their first child. Then time rolled forward and he was teaching a little son to ride while a toddler played in the wildflowers, her brown hair dancing in the wind. Aumaleigh would smile, holding another baby in her arms.

Happiness. That was his future. His chest ached with the power of it. He blinked, and that future faded from his mind but it was not gone. It had taken root in his heart.

"Good afternoon, Gabriel." Aumaleigh sat perfectly balanced on the top rail, her smile so lovely it blinded him to all else.

Just like that, he was in love with her. He was going to love her with all he had for the rest of his days.

"Uh, Uncle Gabriel?" Seth's voice intruded, dragging Gabriel out of the bright, hot sun of the memory and into the damp icy rain. He blinked, confused. His nephew was studying him curiously. Seth arched a brow. "Did you hear me? I think we have to resort to another tactic. I think there are some boards we can use in Ma's shed. We'll wedge them beneath the runners and muscle the cart out. It's just sinking deeper."

"Fine. You do that." Gabriel felt like a fool, letting the past drag him back like that and take him under. He didn't want to remember what he'd worked so hard to forget. It had taken him more years than he could count to let go of the pain that woman had intentionally caused him. It had taken a Herculean effort to lay it all to rest. No sense stirring it up now.

Seth took off, leaving Gabriel standing in the cold rain. Lawrence had wandered over to check on his donkey, and Gabriel found himself facing the house Aumaleigh had disappeared into. Did she regret what she'd done, he wondered? She had to have spotted him in the road--she would have been looking right at him when she rode up the street. Was she remembering what they once had?

Maybe he was the only one. That made him sad. He turned his back and leaned on his shovel, waiting for Seth to return.

* * *

Gabriel. He was all Aumaleigh could think about as she unbuckled the saddle bag in the warmth of Adam's parlor. Rain dripped from the leather and she took care as she extracted the lovingly folded dress.

"I can't believe you want to do this for Annie." Adam swallowed hard, struggling with shyness and deep emotion. He was a good man, a teamster who was building a good business locally after moving here to court dear Annie. He shrugged his burly shoulders. "It will mean a lot to her to wear your wedding dress."

"When I offered it to her, she said no. Not because she didn't want to, I could see that in her eyes plain enough." Aumaleigh's lower lip wobbled thinking of her niece. The poor girl had been through so much, but her luck had turned for the better--no, the very best. Annie and her younger sister Bea were happy living on the Rocking M, and now she was engaged to be married on Saturday. "Annie said she couldn't be responsible for such a costly dress. Now, it's not all that costly. I made it myself so long ago. The most valuable thing I put into it was love, and that's exactly why Annie should wear it. I know she doesn't have money to spare for a wedding dress."

"Are you sure it should come from me?" Adam's forehead furrowed. He studied the dress she spread out on the back of the sofa--the mother-of-pearl buttons, the careful lacework, the dainty cut of sleeves and ruffle. "This comes from you, Aumaleigh. I can't pretend otherwise."

"Then only tell her you have a dress for her to wear. Leave it as a surprise. Deliver it to her the evening before, and she'll have no excuses left. She'll have to wear it." Aumaleigh ran her fingertips across the delicate lace collar, remembering. Her heart filled with the power of memory, with the sweet perfection of love. "She's family, and so far all my other nieces have been married in it. It seems fitting."

"I know she would love it. She's talked to me about the dress." He raked his fingers through his thick, dark hair. The angled line of his jaw worked. "It's generous of you, Aumaleigh. It would save me the cost of a dress, one that wouldn't mean nearly as much to her. I'll buy her a few nice everyday dresses instead."

"That sounds perfect to me." Aumaleigh fished in the bottom of the saddlebag for the matching veil and laid it out too. "I'll come over the morning before the wedding to iron it and give it a few tucks. Annie is shorter than I am."

Adam found that agreeable and offered her coffee or tea to warm up before heading back out into the weather, but she felt restless. Her gaze slid to the window where she could see Gabriel bent over, working with Seth to wedge boards beneath the stuck cart. Poor Lawrence. She felt sorry for that young man.

After waving off Adam's profound thanks, she scurried down the walkway. It wasn't easy keeping her gaze directly ahead of her when her eyes wanted to veer to the right where Gabriel was. Stubborn eyes. She didn't know why they wanted to see him--she certainly didn't. It hurt too much to look at him. He reminded her of what she'd lost and of the decades of emptiness she'd lived through, without a husband and family of her own. She wanted to say that was his fault, too--after he'd hurt her so badly. No way did she want to go near another man again.

But, if she had to be honest, perhaps Mother had a lot to do with that. Always mentioning it, always reminding Aumaleigh of her failure to hold a man's love and attention, that no good man would want a nobody and a nothing like her. By the time she'd gotten over her heartbreak and learned to disregard her mother's words, it had been too late. She'd been far too old for any man to take an interest in her.

It's only regret, she told herself as she turned her back and gathered up her dear mare's reins. Regret hurt, but it didn't mean she wanted to go back and do it over again or make a different decision when her wedding to Gabriel had loomed near. Her chest cinched so tight with pain, she could scarcely breathe. She stuck her foot in the stirrup, bounded upward and landed in the saddle.

The truth was--she wished she'd made a different decision back then. She wished it with all her might, to the bottom of her soul. If only she had the power to reverse time and return to that moment when she'd been so torn and uncertain, haunted by her mother's bitter predictions that had felt so true at the time. So true. When they'd been nothing but hate.

She wasn't sure if it was rain against her cheeks or tears as she reached for the reins knotted over the saddle horn. Somehow her gaze slid to the right and found him. Gabriel had straightened up, hands on his hips, and the twenty yards of street separating them shrank to zero. Her heart lurched in her chest, a gasp rasped up her windpipe and the instant their eyes met, she felt that familiar, decades old twist of recognition in her soul.

I don't love him anymore, she told herself stubbornly, tearing her gaze from his. She swung her mare around in the street, hurrying the animal as fast as she could safely go in the slushy conditions, feeling the piercing weight of Gabriel's gaze on her back. Tears blurred her vision, burning scorching hot even as the wind cooled them.

She could never love him again. Not a man who let her down so thoroughly, not a man she could never trust. But that didn't stop the aching. No, the pain continued on as cold and as relentless as the rain.

* * *

Gabriel knocked the rain from his hat brim, watching Aumaleigh disappear down the street. Slim and elegant, she sat on that horse as if she were a queen on a throne. His throat felt thick as emotion lodged beneath his Adam's apple in a big, uncomfortable lump.

She never married. Josslyn's words came back to him, full of accusation and blame. *What does that tell you? All these years she never moved on. That's what you did to her.*

He blinked, struggling to keep sight of the dove gray color of Aumaleigh's coat through the gunmetal gray rain, but her horse turned a corner, and she was lost to him. He gritted his molars together, clenching his jaw, fighting the strident urge to go tearing down the street after her. He could have sworn she was crying, although he had no proof.

She was the one who'd done the heart breaking. Aumaleigh, and no one else. That old bitterness welled up, but it didn't carry the impact it once had. Frustrated, he hung his head, wishing he hadn't come to town--and wishing he didn't have to go.

CHAPTER ELEVEN

Wind battered the west wall of the schoolhouse, making it unbearably cold as it had been all afternoon. The rainstorm had stopped late Sunday, but bitter cold had set in overnight and stayed for the day. Giving a little shiver, Penelope looked up from marking grades in her book, casting a glance over her students with their heads bent over their studies.

Except for Sadie Gray, naturally. The girl looked far too busy on her slate to be working her assigned arithmetic problems. Not at all surprised, Penelope rose from her chair, circled her desk and ambled slowly down one of the aisles.

Sadie got the message, grabbed her slate cloth and erased whatever she'd been drawing. Like a star pupil, she turned her attention back to the schoolbook open on the desk before her. Penelope strolled closer, surveying each student as she passed. Little Ilsa Collins mouthed words as she read, toiling over her reading assignment. Penelope made a mental note to spend some extra time with her on reading tomorrow morning. Beside her, delicate Kit Redmond turned the page in her reader, hungrily devouring the words. Maybe it would be a good idea to hunt down a novel for Kit to take home. She knew the Redmond family was struggling financially.

One Denby twin looked up from his geography assignment and gave her an innocent, wide-eyed grin as if he could never do anything wrong--nor had he ever. Her suspicions rose and she vowed to keep an eye on him. He might be up to something. She smiled back, ruffled the boy's dark hair and kept going.

"I was studying this time. Honest." Sadie Gray broke the silence and held up her slate. "See? I got two problems done already."

"You would have more done if you hadn't wasted time drawing." She couldn't help smiling at the girl who gave a dramatic sigh, unable to argue, and went back to work.

And then there was Evie. The little girl sat in her ragged dress and worn through shoes. Little goose bumps rose on her forearms where her too short sleeves rode up as she turned the page in her new grade one arithmetic book. How were things going with her and Nathaniel? Penelope had hoped he might pay her a visit on Sunday, but the roads had been terrible and had gotten worse as the day went on, so she wasn't surprised when he didn't come by.

Although Gil delivered both lunch and supper, cooked by Maebry and no doubt requested by Nathaniel. His thoughtfulness gave her a warm feeling. She smiled at Evie and kept strolling down the aisle. Nathaniel's thoughtfulness meant a lot, but wasn't that the way it always was in the beginning? Alexander had been gallant in the beginning, bringing her gifts and doing thoughtful little things.

Troubled, she paced by Bea McPhee's desk, who was bent studiously over her spelling book.

"Uh, Miss Shalvis?" Clarice Breckenridge broke the stillness in a near whisper. "It's time to go home now."

"What?" She whipped around, startled to see the time was five minutes past four. "Sorry, children. I was so pleased with how well you were studying I forgot to watch the time. You may put your books away. School is dismissed for the day."

Chaos ensued. The Dunbar twins hooted and hollered, shoving each other as they launched out of their seats and across the room. They threw open the door with a bang and their boots pounded all the way outside. Girls began to talk, having more decorum as they tidied up before rising properly from their desks. All except for Sadie Gray, who'd charged to the window to check on the weather.

"It looks even icier!" she announced to her group of friends, Evie included. "There's enough to go sliding on. I gotta go home and change into my trousers."

The poor sheriff, Penelope thought as she headed toward her desk.

He was going to have his hands full when that girl came of courting age.

"Miss Shalvis!" Devin Dunbar poked his head around the corner, cheeks red from being outside in the cold. He disappeared, but his voice carried to whomever he was speaking to inside the vestibule. "Yeah, she's in there. Is she in big trouble?"

"No, Devin, your teacher is not in big trouble." The sheriff strolled into sight, his tin badge reflecting in the lamplight "But I have heard things about you and your brother. You two better toe the line. I'd hate to have to haul you boys in."

Devin grinned wide. "I'm gonna be a sheriff when I grow up. My ma says it should put fear into outlaws everywhere."

"Your ma is a wise woman," Milo quipped, ambling in his self-assured way. He was a tall man, well built without being bulky, and while he radiated competence and might, it was overshadowed by his kindness. He tipped his Stetson in a lawman-like way. Good afternoon, Miss Shalvis. I wanted to drop by and update you on my progress, but I don't have good news for you."

"I expected as much." She grabbed a ladder-back chair from the corner. "Please, come sit and get comfortable. Would you like something hot to drink?"

"No thanks, Miss." Milo swept off his hat, rainwater dipping off the brim as he sat down. "I followed the thieves as far as their tracks would let me that night. I ended up out of town about half a mile before they ended."

"I didn't expect to get my things back, and most of it was food." She gathered her skirts and settled into her chair. "Perhaps you should let this go. I worry someone may have simply been hungry."

"That may be, but my experience says otherwise." He grimaced, keeping his voice low so it wouldn't carry to the handful of students gathering up their schoolbooks before heading toward the door. "If it was just the food, I would let this go since you requested it. But the other items taken suggest this could be men on the run from the law, hiding out in one of the abandoned shanties all over this county. Someone might be settling in to stay a while, and I'd like to find them before they do this type of thing again. I hear from Nathaniel that he put better locks on your doors."

"Yes. That should keep me safe from now on." She folded her

hands in her lap. Her heart kicked at Nathaniel's name. "But will other people be at risk?"

"Likely. I'm asking folks to report any new faces they see in town, and I'd like you to do the same. Maybe this was a random thing, but my gut tells me the robbers targeted you." When he shrugged, a rivulet of rainwater sluiced down his sleeve and plopped onto the floor. The poor man looked as if he'd been out in the weather all day. "You didn't leave a beau behind in Boston who was vengeful or violent, did you?"

"No, but you're thinking of what happened with Verbena McPhee, aren't you?" A bad feeling dug into the pit of her stomach and stayed there. She couldn't deny it. "I assure you, the man I left behind wasn't that attached to me."

"I just wanted to check." Milo stood, nodding politely. "I'll be in touch. If you see anything suspicious, or if you see strangers taking an interest in you, tell me. Even if you feel like it's nothing. I want to make sure this doesn't happen to anyone else."

"If you think it's important, I will." She stood, too, no longer feeling so calm about the break-in. "Thank you, Sheriff."

"My pleasure, Miss Shalvis." He swept on his hat and ambled away to speak with his daughters who were waiting for him.

Suddenly she noticed a change in the air. It felt as if the lamplight had brightened. Nathaniel Denby strode into the room. Pleasure whisked through her. Her knees went weak. Her chest seized. It was *good* to see him.

"I finished work early today, so I walked over to meet Evie." Happiness shone in his indigo blue eyes as if he were very glad to see her again. "It's just too bad that I get to see you too."

"Yes, it's really too bad," she agreed, laughing. Nathaniel's gaze fastened on hers, and the way he looked at her, as if he saw everything about her and adored it, was like something out of one of her beloved books. The memory of their second kiss made her blush.

She was already looking forward to kiss number three.

"How are you doing? Concern pinched in the corners of Nathaniel's eyes. "I hope the better locks on the doors gave you peace of mind last night."

"Yes, they certainly did." She adored that he cared, that he was here checking on her. "I'm fine, but the sheriff is taking it seriously. He seems terribly upset."

"That's Milo. He's dedicated to this town." Nathaniel's gaze drifted toward the vestibule doorway where Milo had kneeled down to button up his youngest daughter's coat. Beautiful little Sally chattered away at him, her blond flyaway hair full of static, while her father listened intently. Nathaniel studied the pair for a moment. It was hard to tell what he was thinking when he arched a brow at her. "I had an ulterior motive in coming to pick up Evie."

"Is that so?" Penelope blushed, staring down at her toes. A few students lingered in the classroom, either gathering their books or warming their winter wear in front of the stove before donning them for a long walk home. She did her best to keep her interest in the man hidden from view.

"I was hoping you wanted to have supper with us tonight."

"That is a very generous offer." She peered up at him. "As a schoolteacher, I get invitations to dine at my student's homes all the time."

"I'm not asking the schoolteacher to dinner. I'm asking you." His baritone vibrated low and deep, such a wonderful sound.

Every cell in her body responded. Joy leaped through her, but she tamped it down and did her best not to smile *too* much. "Then I guess I have no choice but to say yes."

"That may not be the wisest answer, since I'm cooking. But I'll do my best not to burn anything or make you ill." He rolled his eyes. Laughter tugged up the corners of his mouth. "You're not trying to think up excuses to get out of it, so I'll take that as a good sign?"

He arched one dark brow, and beneath the humor lurked a more serious question. She read it as easily as words on a page. He was really interested in her. Somehow she managed a nod. After Alexander, she feared no man would want her for who she was. It was a very good sign.

"Then we'll see you in an hour. We'll drop by and pick you up." Nathaniel caught her hand in his and gently squeezed.

Her blood sparkled in her veins. Her soul sighed--like recognizing like. "No, don't go to the trouble. I would be happy to come over on my own. It will save you a trip, since you'll be cooking and all."

"As you wish." He held her hand a moment longer, and she hoped it was because he didn't want to let her go. When he did, her hand tingled, missing his touch long after he'd said his goodbyes and led

Evie out of the schoolhouse.

This feels like it's meant to be. The thought settled into her heart with calm certainty as she wrapped her arms around her middle. *This feels like destiny.*

"Miss Shalvis?" a small voice asked.

She blinked, torn from her thoughts, and smiled down at little Kit Redmond. She took one look at the coat buttons laying in the girl's open palm.

"They just broke off," Kit explained, blinking hard. "I don't know how to fix 'em and I'll freeze up if I can't button my coat all the way. That's what my ma always said."

Tears burned behind Penelope's eyes because she hated that the little girl had recently lost her mother. The poor child. Heart aching, she brushed away one precious tear with the pad of her thumb. "I'm pretty good with a needle and thread. Come over to my desk, and I'll sew those on for you in no time at all."

"Th-thank you, Miss Shalvis. Pa can't sew." Kit sniffled, shoving a strand of hair out of her face.

"If you have any more loose buttons, you can bring them to me any time. I'll tighten them up in a jiffy, okay?" Penelope held out her hand, loving the feeling of the child's fingers closing around hers so trustingly.

Duty called, so she tried to turn her thoughts to the task at hand. She pulled out her bottom drawer and fished through her reticule for her emergency needle and thread. She could barely concentrate enough to sew on the buttons. Her mind kept jumping to the evening ahead and how wonderful it was going to be.

* * *

Fine, he was more than a little nervous. Nathaniel grabbed a dish towel, wrapped it around the oven handle and pulled open the door enough to peek in. The chicken looked almost done, crispy brown on the outside. He eased the door closed, vowing to remember to check on it in a few minutes. Of all nights, tonight was not the time to burn supper. It was no way to impress a lady.

Footsteps tapped closer. Evie hesitated in the kitchen doorway, hands clasped in front of her patched skirt. Her wide, dark blue eyes found his.

"Is Miss Shalvis coming up the walk?" He asked because the girl had been patiently watching out the front window for her teacher.

Evie nodded emphatically.

"Then why don't you go let her in? I'll be there in a minute." He didn't want to leave until he'd checked the potatoes. He grabbed a fork to stab one of them to test it while Evie's shoes padded quickly away. That's when he heard a thud and the girl's gasp. Something wooden clattered to the floor. Glass shattered.

Looked like maybe he'd just lost another lamp.

Utter silence filled the house. He set down the fork, remembering how upset and frightened Evie had been the last time she'd tripped on something. Sympathy rushed through him for the girl, so unsure of herself, not to mention those shoes she insisted on wearing were a hazard. He rushed through the kitchen, into the dining room and skidded to a stop in the entry way hall, with the little side table overturned and the lamp in pieces.

This time they were lucky, it hadn't been lit. Kerosene had spilled all over the floor. The girl lay sprawled on her stomach, momentarily stunned. Panic beat through him because she wasn't getting up. Blood blossomed on her sleeve. She'd cut her hand.

"S-sorry," she stuttered in the quietest of whispers, shocking him.

Before he could stop her, she pushed up onto her knees using both hands. That had to hurt. He rushed to lift her away from the kerosene and broken glass. Her little body stiffened, ready to be shaken hard and beaten. She recoiled, waiting for the blow even after he'd put her down in the front room.

"Sorry," she whispered again, eyes closed, tears leaking from between her lashes. "I'm sorry. Sorry, sorry, sorry."

"I know it was an accident." He knelt before her and tried to grab her wrist so he could get a good look at the cut. Blood sluiced from it, dripping from her fingertips and onto her skirt, turning it crimson red. "What I'm worried about is your hand. You're hurt, Evie."

"No," she whispered stubbornly, jerking her hand away from him and hiding it behind her back. Blood dripped to the floor. *Plop, plop, plop.*

He felt horrible for her, for the pain she was in and for what she'd been through before she'd come to live with him. He pulled a clean handkerchief out of his pocket, shook it open and knelt before the girl. She was so little, just a wisp of a thing, blinking hard against her tears.

"Hold out your hand, Evie." He kept his voice gentle. "I need to look at it. You're bleeding pretty bad."

"It don't hurt none," she rasped so low, he had to lean in to hear it. "Really. I'm okay."

"Do as I say, please." He wasn't going to back down and she heard it in his voice. She sighed, sinking into herself a little more. Tears clung to her eyelashes, but didn't fall.

Her hand was bloody, but there were no visible shards of glass. Nathaniel carefully pressed his handkerchief to her palm and steered her backward into a nearby chair. Out of the corner of his eye, he saw Penelope standing on the porch, staring in at them. The empathy on her beautiful face was the most amazing thing he'd ever seen.

"Sit right here and keep pressure on it." He guided her other hand into place, holding the handkerchief against the streaming blood and climbed to his feet. He felt every bit of Evie's misery all the way to the front door. When he opened it, Penelope stood there, compassion luminous in her hazel eyes.

"Oh, I see there was an accident." She studied the floor, the broken glass and the drops of blood. "Here, take my things. I'm quite good at doctoring."

That didn't surprise him. She thrust her reticule, coat and scarf and a basket of cupcakes (clearly baked by the McPhee sisters--no one made frosting flowers like they did). Without another word, she stormed away and disappeared around the corner.

"Evie, what a brave girl you are." Penelope's voice drifted to him, as sweet as song. "That's a terrible cut and you haven't even made one sob. Here, let me take a look."

"Nooo." The word came twisted, full of whispered pain.

"Trust me, Evie. Please." Love shone in Penelope's voice, and he wanted to believe she felt something special for Evie.

And for him.

He hung up her coat and scarf and circled into the front room. Penelope knelt before the girl, her fingers red with blood.

"Nathaniel, I think we need the doctor." Apology shone in her eyes. "She is going to need stitches. I could do it, but she should have some laudanum for the pain."

"I was going to fetch him." He already had his coat on. "Are you all right if I leave?"

"We'll be fine." Penelope rocked back onto her heels, staring up at the man. She'd never forget the sight of him through the window. She'd stood on that porch unable to take another step, gaping at how tender and caring he was with the child. Tenderness ebbed into her heart, as sweet as poetry.

So, this is what falling in love feels like, she thought, watching him go. Her heart had never felt so big. Finally, real love was happening to her. It was a dream come true.

CHAPTER TWELVE

"Good night, Doc. Thanks for coming by." Nathaniel grasped the doorknob firmly, opening up to the frigid cold outside. The wind gusted in like a warrior with knife bared. "It's a bad night to be out. I'm sorry about that."

"Things happen. You just take good care of that little girl up there. Something tells me she's been through a lot." Doc Hartwell's weathered face wrinkled up, full of concern. "I'll be back to check on her late tomorrow afternoon. Now, she can go to school if she's feeling up to it, but she has to keep that bandage good and dry. Any problems, you know where to find me."

"I do. Have a good night." Nathaniel shivered, closed the door and heard the muffled ring of a pot lid coming from the back of the house. He shook his head, knowing this was the moment of truth. There was no doubt about it. Their first date had been ruined. Supper was burned beyond a crisp and had likely gone cold by now.

"I'm glad I rescued the chicken from the oven when I smelled it burning." Penelope opened the oven door to check on whatever was inside (it smelled like warming charred chicken). "I'm not sure how it will taste re-heated. I cut off the black parts and it's almost warm now."

"That's beyond the call of duty, Penelope." Wearily he ambled into the kitchen. "You're the guest. You're not supposed to be cooking."

"Technically, I'm only re-heating." She tossed him a genteel smile, softly radiant.

This was not a woman who made a fuss when things didn't go according to plan. No, she was far too classy and completely, incredibly out of his league. But look at her standing there, at ease here. It was simple to imagine her cooking at the stove for real, day in and day out. Aching filled his chest. Powerful wanting rose up. He'd never needed anything before the way he needed her. He wanted to keep her here forever. He didn't know how to tell her, but surely she could tell what she meant to him.

"You still shouldn't be doing it. This is my kitchen, so it's my job." He sidled up behind her, breathing in the soft floral notes of her perfume and the feminine warmth of her hair. He reached around her to take the wooden spoon from her to give the cubed potatoes a push around the fry pan. He'd been lonely for so long, but that was over now. He knew it down to his soul. "Why don't you go pour yourself a cup of tea and relax at the table? I'll finish up here."

"I'm not sure I can trust you not to burn the potatoes," she teased. "Maybe I'd better stay."

"Well, maybe you're right." He wrapped his arms around her more tightly, moving in to bring her flush against his body. His heart skipped a beat. It was so wonderful holding her like this. He wanted to let his eyes drift shut hang onto her all evening long, but, honestly, he'd already burned supper once. He feared she would hold it against him if he did it a second time. "My mind seems to be on something other than the potatoes."

"I noticed."

"Probably because there's a beautiful woman in my kitchen."

"Really, where?" She pretended to glance around, making them both laugh, but, honestly, it felt good to know he thought she was beautiful. "Perhaps you need new glasses."

"Could be. I'll have to look into it." He gave the potatoes a stir, and they sizzled in the melted butter, smelling delicious. He lifted the pan from the stove and set it on a hot pad on the counter, but he didn't move. Not one inch. "In the meantime, I don't want to let you go."

"That would be all right with me." She turned in his arms, facing him, more vulnerable than she'd ever been. There her heart went, opening wide again and brimming with feeling--feeling for him. She blushed, because she'd never felt so close to anyone before. It was thrilling.

It was terrifying.

Down deep, she feared he might get to know her, really know her, and change his mind about her. That, like Alexander, he couldn't come to love her after all. But those were only her fears--fears she could defeat. She swallowed hard, lifting her chin, vowing not to let her fears stop this moment--this possibility. True love only happened if you risked your heart. She'd learned that from dozens of books. You couldn't win what you didn't risk.

"I care for you so much, Penelope." Affection for her lit up his eyes. Nothing had ever been so mesmerizing. "I keep telling myself not to follow my feelings. That's dangerous ground. It never works out for me."

"I know what you mean." They really were kindred spirits, made of the same heart. Gratitude burned beyond her eyes. She really had found the right man, the man of her dreams. She splayed her hands on the span of his chest (so iron-strong, so male-hot) and let go of her fears. "We've both been unlucky in love. Maybe our luck is about to change."

"I think so, too." Sincerity turned his eyes to a striking blue-black. "You're an incredibly beautiful woman. Don't think I didn't notice that right away. But at heart, you are even more lovely. The way you are with your students, the kindness you show your friends, and how you've been to Evie--" He didn't finish his sentence, just swallowed hard.

Tears pooled in her eyes. No one had ever said anything like that to her before. He made her feel beautiful for the first time--he made her feel wanted. Truly wanted. She let her fingertips curl into his shirt, so overcome with feeling she pressed a kiss to his lips, hoping he could feel every bit of affection in her soul.

He returned the kiss. His mouth caressed hers tenderly, with a blissful reverence that told her just how deeply he felt. As if from very far away an almost scorched, burnt smell permeated her senses. She broke the kiss and sniffed the air.

"The chicken!" Nathaniel laughed, rolling his eyes. "Let's hope we've rescued it in time."

He grabbed a dishtowel and hauled open the oven door. Only the outside pieces on the platter had been crisped, so not too bad.

"I'll take those," he said amiably. "Before this goes any farther between us, I have to know one thing. Are you a good cook?"

"I've never had any complaints."

"That's good, because one of us had better be or we'll starve." He closed the oven door jauntily and went in search of three plates, but his words had forever changed things.

He was thinking of a future together, too. A serious future. She smiled. Forever with him would be the best future she could imagine. The very best.

* * *

"She's asleep." Nathaniel's whisper carried into Evie's upstairs doorway where Penelope stood, shrugging into her coat. His gaze narrowed as he rose from the chair beside Evie's bed, put his book down on a side table and crossed the room. "I was just going to come down and find you. You're going home?"

He didn't sound happy about that. Penelope had to admit it felt nice. She wanted to stay and talk and read, just as they'd been doing all evening. She wanted to be in his presence. Regretfully, she drew her coat's sash tight around her waist and tied it. "It's getting late, and I have school tomorrow."

"Right." He closed Evie's door and followed her down the hall. "It was a nice evening, in spite of everything."

"My ma always used to say, it's not what you do but who you are with that makes the moment." Penelope sighed, feeling the twist of sadness that her mother wasn't here to meet Nathaniel. She would have loved him. She headed down the stairs, gripping the banister. "All that matters is that I got to spend time with you and Evie."

"In her room, eating slightly scorched chicken." Good humor rang in his voice. "It wasn't exactly a classy evening."

"Well, we did spend time taking turns reading *The Pickwick Papers* out loud." Penelope touched down, swished into the parlor and admired his wall of bookcases (full of books, of course). "It's my favorite way to spend time."

"Mine, too." He came to a stop beside her. "Evie is doing better, don't you think? I mean, she's talking."

"Whispering, but it's a start." She reached into her coat pockets to draw out her knit hat. "The way you took care of her tonight really mattered to her. You were so loving, Nathaniel. You showed her you are someone she can count on to treat her well and to care for her."

"How could I not care for her? She's a good girl." His jaw worked.

Muscles corded in his neck. "I hate to think what she's been through."

"Exactly how I feel." She tugged on her hat and adjusted it, her chest heavy with sadness for the girl. "You've made a big difference for her."

"Me? No, I'm doing what anyone would do." He waved off her compliment humbly. "I think it's you who has made the difference. She comes home from school a little happier every day. You were so kind to her tonight. You're a gift to her."

"Well, I *am* a pretty good teacher," she quipped, blushing because his words touched her. They mattered. She worked hard at her job, but she knew that wasn't what he meant. He meant tonight. He meant personally. She pulled her gloves out of her pocket, feeling so close to him emotionally--and never wanting that closeness to end.

"You know I'm coming courting, right?" He took her gloves and put them on her.

What an incredibly sweet thing to do. She watched him work the knit wool over her fingers and swallowed hard against the rising lump in her throat. "Well, I suppose I'll answer the door when you knock."

"That's a relief. I was worried." The sparkles in his dark blue eyes said otherwise. What looked like affection glittered there, so precious. The most precious thing of all.

Her chest squeezed hard. She felt brimming over, she felt too full, her emotions so bright they seemed to outshine her. She took a step toward the door, closer to Nathaniel.

"Wait here one minute." He drew her into his arms for a kiss. Sweet and quick but full of feeling. He stepped back, reaching for his coat. "I'll run next door and ask the neighbor to watch Evie while I take you home."

"No, you should stay with her." She shook her head adamantly, thinking of the little girl upstairs. "She needs the security of knowing you're here."

"She's asleep. She won't know," he argued, firmly.

But it didn't matter. Penelope shook her head, her mind made up and whipped open the door. She hopped outside into the bracing cold. "Too late. Besides, if you leave Evie right now, I'll hold it against you."

"If I don't see you safely home, I'll hold it against myself."

"You can make it up to me later." She hardly felt the bitter wind buffeting against her as she padded down the icy walkway. "Maybe we could have a meal that isn't burned?"

"Perfect," he called out.

Yes, that was the word, she thought as she trudged into the dark, lonely stretch of street. Perfect. Meant to be.

She wrapped her arms around her middle, trying to keep the happiness in. It was incredible how life worked out. When she'd arrived here in September, she'd never felt so lonely. Cut off from her family, disowned by her father, heartbroken by a one-sided romance. Her father had said she'd never make it, but look at her life. She had a wonderful job, a cute little home, new friends she treasured and now she was being courted. *Really* courted by a man who looked at her with love.

"Miss Shalvis?" A rather superior voice called out in the night. "Is that you?"

She glanced over her shoulder, spotting a woman standing in her open doorway, draped in a heavy shawl. Penelope cringed but put on her most pleasant smile. "Why, hello, Mrs. Crabtree. How are you this evening?"

"You mean, night. It's past nine o'clock. It's officially nighttime and yet you seem to be out and about being entertained by a man unchaperoned after hours." Maude Crabtree set her pointy chin. "It's shameful, that's what it is."

"I was having supper with Nathaniel Denby and his young niece." She came to a stop in the road. An icy chill raced through her. She had a bad feeling about this. "It wasn't as if we were alone. Nothing improper happened, I assure you."

"You are my children's teacher. You are an example of good morals and proper behavior." Maude marched down her sagging porch steps and stopped at the bottom one. She drew herself up to her full height. "The superintendent will hear about this, mark my words. This time that scoundrel of a lawyer won't change my mind."

"I'm sorry to hear that, Mrs. Crabtree." She blew out a sigh, hoping it would deflate the jittery feeling inside her chest. It didn't. "Evie cut her hand, and I stayed to help out. It's my fault entirely that I lost track of time."

"The excuse doesn't matter. You violated your contract, and good riddance, too." Maude's face pruned unpleasantly. "I never liked them hiring a fancy Boston lady with your airs. I want my girls to learn from someone who knows what life is about. Someone who has everyday values."

"I see." She took a step, nodding slowly. Well, she had to hope the superintendent would understand. She'd done nothing to be ashamed about. "Good night, ma'am."

Only stony silence answered. Penelope could feel the woman's glare, like cold radiating off a glacier as she trudged off into the dark. Her stomach went cold with worry.

"Penelope?" A shadow emerged from around a corner. It was Magnolia McPhee in a cute little sleigh driving Marlowe, her sweet old gelding. Two lanterns swung on poles, tossing light onto the snow and onto Magnolia tucked cozily beneath heavy buffalo robes. "What are you doing out on a night like this? Wait, let me guess. Is it romantic? Does it have to do with a certain handsome lawyer?"

"I may as well admit the truth, because it's likely to be all around town by tomorrow." She shrugged, rolled her eyes and managed a genuine smile. "I had a surprisingly wonderful evening with Nathaniel and Evie, even though it was horrible at the same time."

"Ooh, that sounds intriguing." Magnolia patted the seat beside her. "Climb in, I'll give you a ride home and you can tell me all about it. If you don't, I won't be able to sleep. I'm just a tad nosy."

"No, I don't believe that for a moment," Penelope teased, heading toward the sleigh. "I accept your generous offer. Honestly, I'm just bursting to tell someone about it."

"Excellent, as I'm just bursting to know what's going on." In her merry manner, Magnolia tossed aside the buffalo robes so Penelope could snuggle in beneath them.

She plopped down, settled back against the seat and drew the toasty robes over her. Heat radiated up from the warming irons placed on the floorboards. So comfortable. She stopped shivering, but the bad feeling clenching up her stomach didn't lessen. She glanced over her shoulder, but Mrs. Crabtree's house was no longer in view.

"Let's go, sweet Marlowe!" Magnolia sang out, lightly shaking the reins she held. "I'm just coming back from supper at Tyler's mother's house. Completely a disaster."

"Now I'm intrigued." Penelope leaned closer. "Was it because of Tyler's mother?"

"Oh, no! I want to hear about your evening first." Magnolia's chin went up in the air, sweetly stubborn. "So, what was wonderful? What was horrible?"

"Evie fell and cut her hand pretty bad." Penelope remembered how brave the girl had been, shedding not a single tear over the pain, even when the doctor picked tiny pieces of glass out of her wound before stitching it. Instead, the girl had cried over the expense of the doctor and of the broken lamp. Heartbreaking.

Penelope drew in a deep breath, remembering how sweet it had been to take care of the girl almost the way a real mother would. Fixing her supper plate, making sure she ate, tucking her into bed and reading to her. It had been incredibly sweet. "Instead of the supper Nathaniel had planned, we ended up having a picnic in Evie's room and reading Charles Dickens. That part was wonderful."

"How is that poor little girl doing?" Concern puckered Magnolia's brow. "I've seen her walking to school when I've been zipping around on my deliveries. Why doesn't Nathaniel spring for some nice clothes? Wait! We could sew her up some. We have Annie's wedding to finish sewing for, but that will be all over in a few days. We could do it."

And that was why she loved the McPhee sisters so much. They were the best possible friends. Penelope slipped an arm around Magnolia's shoulders to give her a quick hug. "Thanks for that offer, I'm sure Nathaniel would be touched, but he did buy her new things. She refuses to wear them."

"Aw. That's breaking my heart. I have to do something for her." Magnolia bit her bottom lip, guiding Marlowe around the next corner. "I know. Chocolate cupcakes. That always makes a girl feel better."

"I'm sure she would love that." She remembered how Evie had lit up at the cupcake she'd had for dessert. Penelope was glad she'd brought them. "I've heard chocolate has great healing properties."

"I've heard that too," Magnolia teased back. "Especially chocolate cupcakes with thick chocolate frosting. We'll get right on it. So, what was the wonderful part of the evening?"

"That I was with Nathaniel." That's all it took to fill her with joy. "Just being with him is enough."

"That's how you know he's the one." Magnolia sighed dreamily. "When spending time with him is the best thing there is. Even when things go wrong, he is what's right."

"Exactly." Penelope sighed, too. She couldn't help it. "I thought people only felt this way in books. I didn't expect it to happen for me. So, what went wrong for you tonight?"

"Well, you know Tyler's mother doesn't like me." Magnolia leaned in conspiratorially. "Okay, that's not news. Everybody knows she is totally disappointed in having me as a future daughter-in-law. Anyway, we were discussing wedding plans over supper at their house. She isn't happy that I want a spring wedding, but Tyler told her that's the way it is going to be. Then she proceeded to tell me all about the wedding dress she saw in one of her lady's magazines. It is quite fashionable and she wants the best for her son. Apparently even his bride's wedding dress must be up to a certain standard."

"Uh oh, I see where this is going," Penelope sympathized.

"Yes, she is aghast, simply aghast (I'm quoting her here), that I would want to wear an old, used, out-of-style wedding dress. That was *home-sewn.*" Magnolia rolled her eyes adorably. "That seemed to be the biggest crime of all."

"Did Tyler stand up for you over the dress?" Penelope asked, although she already knew the answer. Of course he had. Anyone could see with one glance how deeply down-to-earth Tyler Montgomery adored and treasured Magnolia.

"Tyler said it was the only dress he wanted to see me in on our wedding day." Pride and love shone in her voice. "It was Aumaleigh's dress, the one she never got to wear. There's something about it, I swear there is. You touch it and you can feel the love she put into it and every single one of her dreams. And then right there in the dining room while the maid was serving dessert, I informed them all that it would be Aumaleigh's dress or I walk down the aisle in my chemise and petticoats. It was her choice."

"Mrs. Montgomery must have been horrified by that." Penelope gave a soft chuckle, imagining the wealthy, very proper matron gasping at the thought.

"Horrified?" Magnolia laughed. "Oh, no. She nearly fell off her chair in a cold faint. The butler had to run and fetch her smelling salts."

"So, in other words, you won?"

"I did." Laughing, Magnolia drew dear old Marlowe to a stop. "I'm really glad you have Nathaniel, Penelope. I've never seen you happy like this."

"It's because I've never been happy like this." It felt as if all the pieces of her life were falling into place, that, like a puzzle, she could see the picture that her life was meant to be. She slipped out from beneath the buffalo robes, careful to keep the warm air trapped for Magnolia. "Thanks for the ride. Have a wonderful rest of your evening."

"You too!" Magnolia snapped the reins and Marlowe took off, dutifully taking his mistress home. "Don't forget we're not having our sewing get together on Saturday."

"Because of the wedding, I know," Penelope called out as Magnolia's sleigh sped away, leaving her alone in front of her little dark house.

She tilted her head to one side, pondering a question. Would she be the next one to start planning her wedding? She tapped down her walk, letting her hope guide her. Her life was full of new possibilities now that Nathaniel was officially courting her.

Nothing could be better than that.

CHAPTER THIRTEEN

The house didn't feel the same without Penelope in it. In the spare bedroom he used as a home office, Nathaniel set down his quill. In fact, from the moment she'd walked out the door last night, something was missing. There was a void, an emptiness. Without her, nothing felt right.

That showed just how deeply he cared about her. Nathaniel rubbed his eyes, strained from spending the past few hours doing nothing but writing contracts for the county commissioner. He glanced at the clock on the wall, surprised that it was almost noon. Time to check on Evie and fix her lunch. He pushed out of his chair and crossed the room, wondering how Penelope's day was going. She was probably seated at her desk, maybe listening to her students' lessons, looking just as lovely and radiant as she had last night.

He warmed from head to toe, remembering their kiss. They were courting now. Pride filled his chest as he ambled across the hallway and pushed open Evie's cracked door. She lay sprawled across her bed, propped up with pillows and covered by an afghan. Her injured hand was elevated on its own pillow.

"I was going to head down and make us something to eat." He leaned against the doorframe. "Do you want to come downstairs with me?"

"Okay," she whispered, sitting up and pushing off the afghan. She looked like a pixie with her long lashes, thick hair with a touch of curl and her round, sweet face. She hopped to her feet, her stockings nearly silent on the wood floor. "Uncle Nathaniel? Do you like Penelope?" She trailed him down the hall.

"Sure I do. Very, very much." He headed down the stairs, doing his best to sound like a level-headed man. "How about you?"

"Yes. She's nice, and she's a good reader." Evie nodded once emphatically as if she thought that was the best of all attributes. "Are you gonna marry her?"

"I suppose in the end that's up to Penelope." He turned the corner, passing through the dining room. "But I hope so."

"Oh." Evie fell silent, hardly more than a shadow as she followed him into the kitchen. She went straight to the counter, bobbed up on her tiptoes and reached for the breadboard.

"I told you. No chores for you today." He whisked it away from her, set it down and opened the bread box. "We want to let your hand rest and heal."

"But I gotta help. I haven't been doing any chores here." Her voice was so small as she bowed her head, staring hard at the hole in her stocking. A little pink toe poked through. She pulled out the knife drawer. "Chores are how you earn your place."

"That's not the way it is here, remember? We went through this at breakfast." He pulled the bread knife out before she could reach for it. "Go ahead and sit down by the stove where it's warmest."

Evie bit her bottom lip, turned around and slowly made her way across the room. A snail could move faster. She tucked her injured hand, encased in a thick white bandage, against her middle, cradled by her good hand. It was the only sign she gave that she was in a lot of pain.

He cut slices from the loaf, layered on last night's leftover chicken (it was a little dry and charred) and spread on some tangy tomato preserves. A noise made him look up. "What are you doing?"

"Getting some wood for the stove." She froze in the middle of lifting a small wedge of split cedar. Her pale face went paler.

"Leave the wood alone." He kept his voice gentle as he sliced the sandwiches in half and loaded them on two plates. "If you want to help, then do me a favor and sit down."

"That's not doin' anything." Distress raised her whisper up in pitch. "If you don't do 'em in the morning, you gotta do twice as many later."

"Where did you learn that?" He grabbed a bowl of cut vegetables from the pantry and dropped sliced carrots, celery and radish onto both plates. "I don't think I've heard that rule before."

"It's the Missus's rule." Evie eased onto the edge of the chair seat. Her eyes turned sad. Very sad.

Concerned, he grabbed two cups from the cabinet. "Who's the Missus?"

"Uncle's wife." Evie's voice grew even smaller. She stared hard at the floor, her shoulders slumping. "She's in charge of me."

"She used to be in charge of you." Everything was becoming clear. "Did she used to give you a lot of chores?"

"No. Well--" Evie bit her bottom lip, pure innocence as she sighed. "It used to feel like a lot, but the Missus said it wasn't. I had to earn my keep, but I'm not earnin' it now cuz of my hand."

She curled into herself, so sorrowful he didn't know what to say. He had no idea she thought this way. Tears filled her eyes.

"That's not the way things work here." He grabbed the milk pitcher and filled her cup. A mix of pity and anger rose up, powerful enough to blind him. He'd sure like to give a piece of his mind to that woman who'd worked Evie to the bone. "If you want to earn your keep here, you need to do your best in school. That's what would make me happy. I know it's what your ma would have wanted."

Evie fell silent, maybe mulling over all that he'd said. She took the plate he offered her. He set her cup of milk on the counter beside her. She stared at her sandwich. "What was my ma like?"

"Don't you remember her?" He knelt to ease open the stove door and check on the fire.

"Sometimes I can't remember her at all." Evie gave a long sigh. Sorrow hung in the air.

He knew exactly how it felt to lose a mother. A mother was a small child's world. Considering how to answer, he grabbed a few pieces of cedar to feed the fire. "Your ma's favorite color was blue. Her favorite time of the year was summer. She used to climb up in the apple tree behind our house when the apples were ripe, pick a branch to hunker down on and get comfortable and eat every apple she could reach. When she was about your age, she used to skip everywhere she went."

"I remember that she was nice." Evie set her plate on her lap and picked up one half of her sandwich with her good hand. "Penelope's nice too."

"Yes, she is." He added another chunk of cedar to the fire and latched the door. He longed to see her again. She was the nicest person he'd ever met.

"If you marry her, I could do lots of chores for her." Evie lit with hope. "I could clean the kitchen and mop the floors. I could get all the food ready to cook and then cook it. I even do the laundry all by myself. I can clean out your stable. I can slop the pigs and feed the chickens if you get any." She arched a hopeful brow at him.

So much hope shone in her eyes, his knees went weak and he couldn't stand up. He knelt there, his throat tight and his chest aching. She really didn't understand what he'd said about school being more important than chores. "I don't want you to worry about all that because if I'm lucky enough to marry Penelope, I'll still keep you around. After all, you're the reason I'm courting her."

"I am?" Evie's head came up. "Really?"

"You're the one who brought us together." Love filled his heart for the girl, growing ever deeper. A month ago, he never would have imagined he'd be raising a child and courting the most beautiful woman in town. His lonely life, his quiet evenings spent alone in this house--all that was over.

He cleared his throat, although when he spoke his voice was gruff. "Eat your lunch. Afterwards, I can read to you for a while if you want or if you're up to it, I can take you to school for the rest of the day. Your choice."

Evie nodded and took a bite of her sandwich. He pushed to his feet, and a knock sounded on the front door.

"I'll be right back," he said, wishing more than anything that it would be Penelope on his front step, even when he knew she couldn't leave the schoolhouse unattended. It just proved how much he missed her. Already she was a part of his life--a part of his heart. He whipped open the door.

"Cupcake delivery." Iris McPhee held up a pink bakery box. "Magnolia heard about your niece's injury and thought these might lift her spirits."

"Well, this is a surprise." But a kind one. "She had one of your cupcakes last night and loved it. Penelope brought them over. Let me grab my billfold."

"Don't even try." Iris shoved the box at him, forcing him to take it. "This is our treat. What are a few cupcakes between friends? You helped us so much with our grandmother's inheritance."

"I was just doing my job is all." He couldn't help inhaling the cupcake aroma. Chocolate. Heavenly. His mouth watered.

"You can't pay me for this, so don't even try." Iris pushed a lock of strawberry blond hair back up beneath the brim of her hat. "Just take good care of your niece. It must feel wonderful to have her living with you."

"I wouldn't trade her for anything. Not even your cupcakes, Iris." He blushed, not knowing how to say what he truly felt. "I'm surprised you're out doing deliveries."

"Magnolia talked me into it, since she and Rose are busy over at the storefront." She grimaced, like a woman expecting the worst. "They are expecting me about now, so I'd better go and see where they've had Tyler's men put the walls. I fear disaster."

He was laughing as she tapped off. He closed the door, the bakery box in hand. Life was full of change and hardship, he reflected as he wound his way back to the kitchen and Evie. But it was full of so much sweetness. Cupcakes, friends, children and love.

He couldn't wait until he had Penelope over again. Maybe this time he wouldn't burn the dinner--a man could always hope.

* * *

At the edge of town, Iris McPhee pulled back on the reins at the hitching post and the mare obliged. Sweet Jane waited patiently, the old dear that she was, while Iris climbed out of the sleigh, slipped her reticule string over her wrist and slid on the icy crust of snow all the way to the post.

"It's about time you showed up." Daisy stepped off the boardwalk behind her, snatched the rein right out of Iris's hand and looped it into a knot. Daisy beamed these days. There was no other way to describe it. Being married to Beckett made her radiate a calm, at ease, totally blissful peace. "Those sisters of ours need some loving guidance."

"Or just a really firm hand and a stick," Iris teased, surprising herself that she could manage to find humor in this situation. She clomped up the steps alongside her sister, narrowing her gaze at the corner shop. A rented storefront! She simply did not approve of this excess spending. "I don't think this is going to turn out well. The town is too small to support a business like this."

"True, but it's making them happy." Daisy paused on the boardwalk, looking through the newly cleaned and glistening front window.

"I can't deny they're happy." Iris squinted at their three younger sisters who were inside laughing and squabbling. Magnolia was shaking a mop at Rose and Verbena. Iris shook her head. "Why did Rose just up and lease this space?"

"Isn't it obvious?" Daisy reached out, took Iris's hand in hers and squeezed lovingly. "She did it for you. Having your own bakery was a dream of yours, right?"

"I can't deny it." Iris's mid-section tensed up. She'd given up on dreams long ago. "It's going to fail. It's going to be a waste of money. It would be better to keep baking in the kitchen at home."

"Sometimes you have to take a risk in life," Daisy smiled sagely. "I almost didn't risk my heart on Beckett. If I hadn't, then I wouldn't be a wife and mother."

"Speaking of Hailie, how is she doing?" Iris adored her new niece. "It's a big change to get a stepmother."

"Yes, but things could not be better with Hailie." Daisy's heart-shaped face went pink with pleasure. "Every time she calls me 'Ma,' I can't believe how lucky I am. Being a stepmother is pretty great."

"You're happy. That's everything I've ever wanted for you." Iris squeezed Daisy's hand in return. "Soon you'll have a baby on the way, and there will be another child to love, another child to call you 'Ma.'"

"Oh, now you're just going to make me cry. I didn't know I could be this happy." Daisy sighed, turning her attention to the window where, on the other side of the glass, Magnolia waved the mop in emphasis to whatever she was saying and Rose and Verbena shook their heads, laughing.

Whatever they were discussing, it might be wiser just to stay out here on the boardwalk and let them hash it out. Except for one thing. It was horrifically cold standing in the blasting north wind.

"Let's go get some tea," Daisy invited, leading the way to the door. "I'm finally done crocheting Annie and Adam's wedding gift."

"I've been frantically knitting, but I still have a ways to go. I need to really work at it the next few evenings." Iris stepped through the doorway and closed the door behind her. She blinked, stunned to see the soft cream walls with dainty, tiny sprays of rosebuds and ribbons.

A new potbellied stove sat in the corner, radiating heat. A gleaming oak and glass counter marched across the shop, cutting it in two. A glass bakery display sat on the end of the counter, completing it. Crystal glimmered in the wall mounted lamps. "Oh, this is just--Daisy, you should have prepared me for this."

"Surprise!" Rose stopped merrily arguing with her sisters and breezed over, adorable with her blond curls bouncing around her oval face. She radiated happiness, too. Being courted by Seth Daniels certainly agreed with her.

Theirs would be the next engagement in town, Iris wagered. And what a happy event that would be. Every one of her sisters would be well and truly matched, married and starting families of their own.

She didn't think she could run a bakery like this by herself. Especially not when the competing bakery from nearby Deer Springs was trying to gobble up all their business. Remembering the promotional letters the rival bakery had mailed to every household in the area (and a coupon), she had to be practical. They were bound to lose business.

What if they couldn't make ends meet? The thought of dipping into savings carved a pit in the middle of her stomach. She didn't like financial instability. Not even Daisy knew of the many times she'd stretched their meager food dollars for the week by not packing a lunch for herself or feigning an upset stomach and going to bed hungry.

"I went with the wallpaper that you liked, Iris." Rose hugged her, bubbling with excitement. "You were right. The tiny flowers make the room big and airy, but warm at the same time. Tyler made the counter himself. He did a beautiful job, didn't he?"

"Yes." She ran her fingertips across the honeyed wood. Against her will, she had to admit it was superb. Simply everything she'd ever wanted when she'd been dreaming away, working in that little bakery in Chicago. This really was like a dream.

Too bad she'd given up on dreams.

"How much did this cost us?" she asked. She had to be levelheaded and circumspect. Life was better on even ground. When you were sensible, you lessened your risk for failure and hurt.

"Stop worrying about money." Rose waved her hand, dismissing the very valid and practical concern of money. "We have tons of it. Besides, the value of a dream can't be measured with dollars and cents."

"I just wish you had some more of that." Iris bit her lip, trying not to let a smile show.

"More of what? Money?" Rose crinkled her brow.

"Sense. Cents. Get it?" Call it a weakness, but she loved a good pun. "When will this be ready for business?"

"I thought you didn't approve." Verbena waltzed over, full of mischief.

"I don't." Iris lifted her chin, biting the inside of her lip to keep her smile firmly hidden. "But since the lease is signed and no one but me wants to break it, we might as well work to make this as little of a loss as possible."

"I like your positive outlook," Magnolia teased. "What if you're wrong? What if we make a profit?"

"Who cares about a profit," Rose piped up. "This is about us working together in our own bakery. This is about the people we hire who will need those jobs. Remember how that felt when we needed work so badly?"

"I do," Verbena spoke up.

"I'll never forget," Daisy agreed.

"Nor I." Iris swallowed hard against the lump building in her throat. Now she understood what this was about. This wasn't about their dreams or their profits as much as it was about helping others. There weren't a lot of job opportunities in a town like this. When the bakery opened, they would need employees. And there were people in this town in desperate need of work.

A knock sounded on the door. Rhoda Collins stood at the door, with a knit wool cap hiding her blond hair. She was still a young woman, but stress and hardship had begun to etch worry lines into her pretty face. A few strands of gray shone in her golden hair.

"Hello, McPhee sisters," she said, looking nervous and shy as she hesitated in the doorway. "I just heard the good news about your bakery and I was, well, I was wondering if--if you would be hiring anyone. I've never worked before outside my home, but I have cooked and baked all my life. Well, you may not be hiring at all, but I just had to ask."

"I'm so glad you came by. Why don't you come in?" Iris remembered all that their dear friend Penelope had said about the Collins family back when they'd been making Christmas gift baskets for the poorest families in town, those in desperate need. Mr. Collins had died in an accident on their farm, the bank had taken back their property and

Mrs. Collins had nothing but the horses to sell for income. How long that money would last a family of three, she didn't know, but it couldn't go far.

Iris pursed her lips, thinking. Anyone could see how sincere of a woman Rhoda was. How worried she must be, wondering how to support her two daughters. Okay, so now she saw the wisdom of Rose's decision and she would embrace it full force. How could she not? They would simply need to make this a profitable endeavor, that was all.

"Rhoda, we will definitely be hiring," Iris said with authority. "You are exactly the kind of employee we need. Daisy, could you pour Mrs. Collins a cup of tea? Let's sit down by the stove and talk."

Rose clasped her hands excitedly. Daisy spun around to the steeping teapot next to the potbellied stove. Verbena grabbed a couple ladder-back chairs from behind the counter. Magnolia unpacked cups from the basket she'd brought, and Iris blinked hard against the sting in her eyes. Just when she was losing every sister she had to romance (and wonderfully so), she had a purpose again.

CHAPTER FOURTEEN

Penelope couldn't remember a school day ever being so long. When the big hand hit twelve and the little hand was on four, she stood up to dismiss the class. Chaos erupted, kids went in every direction and she happily smiled at Evie who was packing up her books one-handed, with Sadie's help.

It was a good sign that Evie had made the second half of the day, and it was easy to see why she'd returned. She and Sadie were fast friends. Plus, it was easy to see that Evie seemed a little happier this afternoon, despite her thickly bandaged hand. That was progress. Maybe one day the girl would be laughing and running around and sparkling like all the other children.

"Miss Shalvis?" Ilsa Collins, the little red haired pixie, hopped over to tug on Penelope's skirt. Her big, round eyes stared up, full of sweetness. She thrust out her hand. "I made something for you. All by myself."

"You did?" Penelope knelt down so she was eye-level with the child so she could better see what lay scrunched up on that small palm. It was a handkerchief made out of a square of blue linen boarded with inexpertly crocheted edging. The stitches were uneven--some too loose, others too tight, but it was a gift from the heart. "Oh, Ilsa. This is the most beautiful piece of needlework I've seen in a very long time. You are very talented with a crochet needle."

"I know." Ilsa gave a humble shrug. "See? It matches your dress."

"Yes, it surely does. Thank you so much, love." Penelope brushed silken strands of red hair out of the child's face. What a sweetheart.

"You're welcome! Bye!" Ilsa dashed off, shoes knelling on the floorboards all the way to the door where her older sister waited for her. The girls took hands and skipped off, heading home.

Still touched by the gift, Penelope folded up the handkerchief and slipped it into her pocket. She intended to make sure she had it in her pocket every time she wore this dress. She hoped that would make Ilsa happy.

Now, on to the blackboards. She grabbed her board rag and spun around. She caught sight of Sadie and Evie still at their desk. Smiling, she swiped away the day's date and the remnants of the eighth grade's arithmetic lesson. Mrs. Crabtree's son had been in that class. Remembering their unpleasant conversation last night, Penelope shuddered. What if the woman did contact the superintendent? Would she be put on probation? Surely, the man would understand the situation. She wasn't worried about that. It just didn't feel good knowing one of the parents thought poorly of her.

She carefully ran the cloth along the wooden frame, catching every trace of chalk dust. Little girl laughter rang out, echoing in the nearly empty room. When she glanced over her shoulder, Evie and Sadie were leaning together, traipsing down the aisle between desks, giggling.

"Miss Shalvis?" Sadie called out. "Do I really have to turn in lines tomorrow?"

"Yes. The arithmetic class needed the board so you will have to do it as homework. I want to see one hundred sentences written neatly on my desk first thing in the morning." Being stern was the part she hated about her job--the only thing. "Do you remember what you are supposed to write?"

"I will not put a frog on Danny's head ever again." Sadie grinned, unrepentant. "And I really don't have to, because I already have. It was hilarious."

"Remember that just in case Danny decides to retaliate." She tweaked Sadie's delicate, curved chin. Oh, she adored the girl. "If that happens, I don't want to hear a single complaint. Got it?"

"Yeah." Sadie grinned, as if the prospect was an intriguing one. "If I don't put a frog on anyone else's head ever again, do I still have to do the lines?"

"I think you know the answer to that." Penelope accompanied the girls across the room.

"Yes, but a girl's gotta hope." Sadie grabbed her coat from the row of hooks in the vestibule. Her little sister waited by the door. Sally was charming in a pink wool coat. The sisters traipsed off, shouting out goodbyes as they stormed out into the frigid sunshine and slammed the door, leaving Penelope and Evie alone.

"I bet you need some help with your winter wraps." Penelope had come to grab the broom, but reached for the remaining coat instead. The thin wool fabric had worn bare in places, nearly see through. How could any child stay warm in this?

"Thank you, Miss Shalvis." Evie's whisper was so low, she had to lean forward to hear it. The girl stuck her arm in the sleeve, careful of her injury.

"Any time, Evie." Penelope helped her into the other sleeve and settled the garment on her shoulders. "How come you aren't wearing the coat Nathaniel bought for you?"

"Because." Evie turned around.

That wasn't much of an explanation. Penelope buttoned her way from Evie's chin to her hem. "Your uncle wants to take care of you now. He's your family."

"No, he's not." The word seemed to grate out, raspy and jagged. Almost tortured.

"He's your uncle. He's your mother's brother. That makes you family." Penelope reached for Nathaniel's blue striped scarf and looped it around Evie's neck. "I am absolutely certain your uncle loves you very much. Why else would he buy you all those nice warm things? He fixes you meals. He reads to you. That is how you know you belong with him."

"Oh." Evie scrunched up her mouth. Her forehead wrinkled deeply.

Penelope sighed. She'd meant to reassure the girl, not to make her more worried. She rescued the broom leaning in the corner of the closet, trying to think of the right thing to comfort the girl.

"Do you really think Uncle will want me to stay?" Evie gave a hiccup-like gulp and stared hard at the floor.

"I'm certain of it." Penelope's heart simply broke. The poor child. She should not have so many worries.

"Would you want to keep me?" So little that voice, vibrating with need.

"I would definitely want to keep you." Penelope felt her world shift, felt the path of her life turn. "No doubt about it."

"Really?" Evie's head snapped up. Hope lifted her up.

"Really." Penelope felt hopeful, too. Love was happening for both of them--for her and for Evie--and she couldn't be happier. She set aside the broom and took Evie's hands, lost in those enormous gloves. "Do you know what this means? You should wear the clothes Nathaniel bought for you. It will make him happy."

Evie blew out a watery sigh.

"I know what it feels like when something great happens to you." Penelope knew only too well, and of this she was absolutely sure. Being with Nathaniel felt so right. So did helping Evie. She pressed her palm against the girl's appled cheek. She couldn't stop the wash of love sweeping through her. "But nothing is going to happen. You aren't going to lose Nathaniel. It's going to be okay."

"No, it's not." She gulped. "Good things don't happen to me. The Missus said so."

"I don't know who the Missus is, but I want you to trust me. Do you know what? You should wear your new clothes to school tomorrow. I want to see how your happy new life looks on you." Penelope couldn't stop the wash of love sweeping through her. "I'm sure it will be beautiful on you."

Tears filled Evie's eyes. Too overcome to speak, she darted away, bursting through the door and shutting it behind her. Hope filled the air as Penelope grabbed her broom, wrapped her fingers around the handle and started to hum while she swept.

Maybe she would plan a little surprise for this evening. Bring over supper and a new book for Evie. She thought of her copy of *Little Women* tucked on her bookshelf at home. It would be perfect.

Yes, she thought as she worked. She'd found a man who cared about her--just her--and what a marvelous feeling that was.

* * *

Nathaniel looked up from his work when he heard the front door open. He was working from home today and was expecting a client, but instead he recognized the quiet knell of Evie's footsteps echoing in the foyer downstairs. She was home from school. He put down his quill and reached for the cup of coffee steaming on the corner of his desk.

He took a sip of the strong, warming brew, savoring the sweetened coffee taste on his tongue. Footsteps rang louder, coming closer. He took another sip, looking forward to seeing her dear face in the doorway. He wasn't disappointed.

"Uncle?" She peered in at him, a bit peaked due to her injury. "Can I have one of the cupcakes in the kitchen?"

"You sure can. Let me come make you some hot chocolate to go with it." He set down his cup, pushed out of his chair and strode across the room. "How was school this afternoon?"

"Okay. Sadie got in trouble again and had to write lines." Evie followed him into the kitchen--and she wasn't whispering. She was speaking in a normal voice, quiet but normal. "Uncle?"

"Yes?" He opened the bakery box on the counter and put a cupcake on a small plate.

"Can I put on the red dress?" Her voice wobbled, sounding anxious.

Well, wasn't that interesting. He liked the change he saw in the child.

"It's your dress. You can wear it if you want." Smiling, he set the plate on the small round table between the back door and the kitchen window. "Why don't you run upstairs and change now? Hurry. It will give me time to make your hot chocolate."

With an excited nod, Evie took off, dashing across the room and pounding up the stairs. Her shoes tapped a fast rhythm across the ceiling overhead. Well, how about that? It seemed as if things were looking up. Pleased, he grabbed a small sauce pan and the hot chocolate tin. A knock pounded on the front door.

That was probably Travis Montgomery, come for his contracts. All business, Nathaniel marched through the house, flung open the door and blinked when he saw Evie's other uncle on the doorstep. He was a lanky man, bearded and middle-aged. He had the look of a farmer to him, one who was far from prosperous.

His black gaze turned cold. "I've come for the girl."

"That's not going to happen." Instant rage pounded through him, fierce as an attacking bear. He drew himself up, his hands fisting, his jaw clenching. This was the man who'd half-starved Evie. Who dressed her in rags and let his wife work her to the bone. Despicable. "Turn around and ride away. Don't ever come back."

"She's mine. I got a paper from a judge down in Bear Hollow that says so." The man pulled out a folded, worn piece of parchment from his coat pocket.

"I don't care what that says." Nathaniel ground out, rage turning his vision crimson. "You surrendered her, and I'm keeping her."

The other uncle unfolded the paper and held it up. "This here gives me the right to take her back. My wife done had her baby and now there's a passel more work to do than we figured on."

"Congratulations on the baby." Nathaniel whipped the document out of the man's hand, glanced at it (the other uncle's name was Merl McCarthy,) tore it in half and let the pieces fall. "There. That's what I think of your claim."

"You can't do that." Merl snatched up the pieces of paper, rescuing them from the snow. "This is a legal document. Tearin' it up don't make no difference. I still got rights to that girl."

"I say you don't. If you have a problem with that, why don't you look up the local sheriff? But I wouldn't count on the law's help if I were you." Nathaniel heard the muffled drum of Evie's shoes on the stairs, tapping fast and furious, coming closer. Evie. He crowded into the doorway. He wanted the man gone before she could see him. "Go home, McCarthy, and don't come back. Not ever, or you will have a fight on your hands that you will lose."

He'd make sure of that. He'd die to protect that child. Filled with protective fury, he slammed the door shut, but a boot wedged into the doorway, stopping it at the last minute.

"We'll see about that." Merl glared past him, over his shoulder. "Hey there, girl. I've come for ya."

Evie's footsteps came to a stop in the hallway. He could feel her distress. He glanced over his shoulder, realizing he'd already failed her. Her shoulders slumped. Her head went down.

"That's what I thought." Merl gave a self-satisfied nod. Triumph glittered in his cold eyes. "Don't think I haven't asked around town about you. Hear you've taken up with the fancy schoolteacher."

"That's not your business." Nathaniel's jaw snapped so tight, the joint ached. He debated the merits of kicking Merl's foot out of the way so he could close the door. It took all his willpower not to plant a fist in the man's face.

"I know what you're up to. Courting her so you can get a woman to take care of the kid." Merl smirked. "That poor schoolteacher don't know you're using her. She's just a spinster, too desperate to know it."

Merl extracted his foot and tipped his battered hat to Nathaniel. "Oops, I think your little girlfriend might have overheard that."

Rage roiled inside him, so it took a moment to realize what the man had said--and that Penelope had tapped to a stop in the walkway, a basket in hand. The look on her face tore at him. He shook his head, it wasn't true. She knew that. She lifted her chin, a true lady as she stepped aside on the walkway to let Merl pass by.

A single sob echoed in the hallway behind him. When he turned around, Evie had frozen into a statue, shrunken into herself. Her sparkle and her happiness had died.

"Your other uncle is gone, and he's going to stay that way." Nathaniel softened his voice, trying to sound as reassuring as he could. "That dress looks really pretty on you. Penelope is here. C'mon, let's invite her in and get some cupcakes."

Evie had gone silent again.

"Maybe this isn't a good time." Penelope ventured close, speaking in her quiet, composed way.

"That was Evie's other uncle," he explained. "The one who dropped her off."

Penelope didn't comment. She turned away, watching the lanky man approach a sad looking horse who backed away from him. Merl managed to snatch one of the reins and beat him with the knotted ends of it a few times before mounting up. He rode away as fast as the road conditions would allow.

Nathaniel's heart began to beat hard and painful, fierce thuds that seemed to rattle every single rib. "What he said about you, he was just trying to make trouble. He must have heard you coming down the walk."

"I don't put a lot of stock in what a man who harms a child says," Penelope said tightly, hesitating on the door step. But she'd heard the words, and they'd hurt. Very much. Maybe because it touched a sore spot, where she was most vulnerable. "He's clearly the type that enjoys saying hurtful things."

"That's my take on him, too." Nathaniel's voice dipped sincerely. Anyone could see the apology in his eyes. He was truly sorry she'd overheard those unkind words.

She was sorry, too. She would simply have to shrug them off. She knew the truth. Nathaniel was not a man who used people. Maybe the words had hurt because she *was* a spinster. Maybe it was time to admit she wanted a future and a family with Nathaniel more than anything. *Anything*.

She handed over the basket. "I brought supper. All I need to do is put it in the oven to bake. Oh, and I need to whip up some biscuits, but I brought bowls and ingredients and everything."

"Penelope, I love you for that." Nathaniel slipped one arm around her shoulder, drawing her against his side where she most wanted to be. "Come in and let's get you warm. I was about to make hot chocolate for Evie. Would you like some?"

"Of course." Her words grated out of her, cutting like a knife. She'd gone completely numb, feeling nothing when being this close to Nathaniel, being held by him, was a dear dream.

Woodenly she lifted her feet, crossing the threshold into the warm house. *I love you for that*, he'd said. *For that*. He hadn't just said that he'd loved her.

"Let me help you." Gentlemanly, he set down her basket.

His knuckles grazed her cheek as he lifted her scarf from around her neck. She bowed her head, fingers trembling, to tug off her gloves. She fought the doubt burrowing into her heart. She unbuttoned her coat, hardly aware of the buttons. Her eyes burned.

Don't be so picky, she told herself as she worked the last button through its hole. That wasn't what he meant. You know it wasn't. But the whisper of doubt remained.

"Here, I'll hang this up." He moved in, smelling of wood smoke, ink and warm, clean man. His indigo eyes turned darker as he lifted the coat from her shoulders, helping her out of it. When he turned to face her, he was trying to smile and smooth things over. "We even have cupcakes."

"Oh, the McPhee sisters must have dropped by." She tried to laugh, tried to sound normal as she forced her feet to carry her down the hall. "I mentioned it to Magnolia."

"Iris came by with a big pink box. It was truly nice." He adjusted his gait to match hers so they were walking toward the kitchen together. "I hope their storefront is very successful for them."

"Me, too." She blew out a shaky sigh, trying to focus on the conversation. Her doubts were like shadows in a candlelit room, trying to creep in and encroach on the light. She simply wouldn't let them. "I worry about the competing bakery over in Deer Springs that's trying to get their business."

"I suspect the McPhee girls will put up a good fight." He gestured toward the kitchen, waiting for her to walk through the doorway first. "It's going to be a lot more convenient to buy baked goods. Now that I have Evie, I have to think about that kind of thing. If I'm remembering right, she has a birthday coming up in a few months. I'll have to get a cake from them."

"Right." Penelope nodded, but the shaking that had been making her hands tremble had traveled up her arms and into her body. It was foolish, really, letting a few words trouble her like that. This time she'd fallen for a man who was trustworthy and honorable. Their relationship wasn't one-sided. All she had to do was to feel the snap of affection that sparked when he took her hand to help her into the chair by the stove.

"Here, relax and warm up." He flashed his dimples at her as he added milk to a saucepan. "Where did Evie go? She was standing right here a minute ago. I suppose she's upset. I should go check on her."

"Why don't you let me?" The shaking was worse. She pushed herself out of the chair, crossing the room on jellied legs. "You tend to the hot chocolate. It's an important job you have there."

"Right. I'll do my best. I don't want to let my two favorite girls down by making substandard cocoa." He winked, and his appreciation glinted in his rich blue eyes.

See how much he cares for me? She shook her head at herself, at her foolish doubts. Maybe it would be a good idea to take her own advice and expect good things for a change. Determined, she gathered her skirts and climbed the stairs. She found Evie in her room sitting still, as quiet as a ghost, staring at the wall.

"He's gone for good." Penelope swept into the room, wanting to rush up and wrap the girl in her arms and never let go, to love her until every wound in that little heart was gone. Maybe one day, she thought, when the time was right, if this courtship progressed. One day, she hoped she and Evie would be truly family. She knelt down beside the foot of the bed. "That dress looks beautiful on you. The fabric looks so warm and soft. You must be very comfortable in it."

Evie didn't answer. It was hard to tell if she was even breathing.

We all have wounds, Penelope thought, *life is hard on everyone. But the silver lining is that we are not alone.* Around the next bend, there was always sunshine and a new opportunity, always someone who cared.

"Let's go downstairs." She took the child's hand in her own. It was cold.

Evie sighed and climbed to her feet with great resignation.

CHAPTER FIFTEEN

He'd been struggling with a lot of emotions all evening long. Now that supper was done, Nathaniel poured steaming water from the tea kettle into the china teapot, watching the steam rise in the lamplight. It hadn't been an easy evening. Merl's visit had put a damper on everything, even when they'd tried to rise above it.

Nathaniel set down the kettle with a clank on its trivet, his stomach bunching up hard. Evie hadn't spoken a word all evening. Not over cupcakes and hot chocolate, not when she and Penelope measured new curtains for her bedroom (Penelope had offered to make them, she claimed she liked to sew). Over the delicious meal Penelope had cooked, Evie had sat quietly at the table, eating in little mouse-like bites and staring at her plate.

Nathaniel grimaced, feeling a mix of anger and uneasiness. He dropped the tea ball into the steaming water. The fragrant aroma of cinnamon, cloves and chamomile rose up on the steam. He leaned against the counter, jumbled up inside.

He wasn't going to lose Evie, was he? Frowning, he grabbed two cups from the shelf. Merl didn't look like a man who could afford a lawyer, and he'd abandoned the child. But all it took was one judge's bad decision, and he'd lose Evie to Montana Territory or to Merl. Either way would be devastating--and entirely possible.

Overhead, he heard the soft tap of Penelope's shoes on the floorboards, crossing Evie's bedroom. She must have gotten Evie to fall asleep.

It was a homey feeling, listening to Penelope's light steps echo down the stairwell. Nathaniel set two cups onto the counter next to the teapot. Looking on the positive side of things, tonight his house felt full of warmth and love and life. Everything he'd ever wished for, and he'd feared he might never have. Penelope sailed into the room, bringing with her that life and light, making his world shine. His heart filled impossibly full, brimming over with a love so strong it bowled him over. He felt helpless against it.

"She finally fell asleep." Penelope sidled in close against the counter and moved the teapot and cups onto the waiting tray. "I've never seen such a sad child. I tried to tell her she was safe here, that her uncle couldn't take her back, but she kept shaking her head no. She refused to believe me."

"Actually, she's not wrong. Not really." He added the sugar bowl to the tray, breathing in Penelope's light, vanilla and spring scent. It soothed the knot of dread sitting in the pit of his stomach, but it didn't ease it away entirely. "Some judges see children as property and territorial law doesn't refute it. A child belongs to his parents, and child labor is seen as a justifiable way to help parents with the financial hardships of life."

"I saw enough of that back in Boston at the city school I taught at. The poverty was heartbreaking, but the children were precious. All I wanted was to make a difference for them." Radiant with love, Penelope sighed. No beauty could be greater.

Love for her shone within him so boldly, it blotted out everything. He was a helpless man, defenseless against the deep, abiding devotion he felt for her. He picked up the tray, carrying it from the room. "All I want to do is make a difference for Evie."

"And you already have." Penelope's regard filled her voice, making it the sweetest sound he'd ever heard. "You've given her a real home. She has a chance here she wouldn't have had before. She's never really been to school, and now she has the chance at an education. She has love."

"Yes, she does." He set the tray on the coffee table, stepping into the soft sepia glow of the lamplight. Standing in that pool of light, he felt as if there was no dark here, no shadows, no doubt. Just certainty. Just their blooming love. He took her by the hand and sat with her on the sofa. "I'm going to ride to Deer Springs in the morning to speak with the circuit judge."

"What a good idea." She turned toward him, the curve of her face delicate as she gave him an encouraging smile. "Do you know the judge? Surely you've worked with him before?"

"Yes. I've known Judge Quentin for many years." He could barely get the words out. Penelope captivated him. She made him feel as if he could do anything, that this future he was just daring to dream of could come true. That anything was possible. "The judge and I go way back. He's a good man and sympathetic to the plight of orphans."

"Wonderful. What a relief to know that you have someone you can go to, someone you can trust to help you." Penelope reached out with her free hand and covered his. Her soft, silken touch--pure comfort--moved him beyond words. He sat a moment, his hands joined with hers, his heart so full of feeling he feared it would burst.

"I have been in a terrible upset ever since that other man left. What a terrible uncle he must have been to her." Penelope shuddered, compassion for the girl (no, it was love for the girl) so tender upon her beautiful face that he lost all sense, all reason.

"Yes," he agreed, hating what Evie had been through. "From what I can tell, he and his wife used her for slave labor around their home and their farm."

"When she should be in school," Penelope added. "She's smart and has a gift with numbers. Surely your judge friend will see right off how much better off she is with you. I could write a letter of recommendation for you, if that would help."

"Very much." He rasped the words out, his throat so tight with emotion he could barely speak. To see her love for Evie, to see her true caring overwhelmed him. This wonderful woman truly cared for him, she'd chosen him. *Him.* Pride, gratefulness and joy twisted up inside him, driving out every last bit of doubt. He knew what he needed to do.

Love glinted in her eyes, as mesmerizing as starlight, as true as dreams. She leaned in to kiss his cheek. "You are such a good man, Nathaniel Denby. Evie is lucky to have you and so am I."

"Marry me." The words popped out straight from his heart. Surprise rushed through him, but then he realized he had never meant anything more.

"Marry you?" Surprise widened her eyes. Her jaw dropped. "I--uh, did I hear you correctly?"

"I know, it's sudden." He was on a rush now, talking fast, holding her hand more tightly, squaring his shoulders. "But I've been waiting for you forever. You can't deny that we have a strong attachment, you and I. We know how this is going to end. I am going to propose and we'll marry one day. Right?"

"Well, I--" She searched for words, trying to get her stunned brain to think. She felt in a whirl--this sudden proposal, his confession that he wanted her. Dazed, she gave a small, slightly hysterical laugh. "But we've just started out. There's so much I don't know about you. Like your middle name, for instance--"

"James," he told her smoothly, certainly.

"--or where you grew up," she finished.

"In a little town called Bend, Pennsylvania." He smiled, leaning in to capture her lips with his. It was a quick kiss, sweet and just a few satin strokes before he broke off, staring deeply into her eyes. Happiness brought out his dimples. "See? That was easy. We have all the time in the world to talk about our pasts. We already know what really matters. At least I do."

"Really?" She swallowed, feeling nervous now and excited. Her lips hummed from his kiss. His hands enfolding hers were warm, steady and sure.

"Here's what I know about you. You are the most amazing woman I've ever met." His sincerity rumbled low and deep, all the way from his soul. "You are beautiful and compassionate and kind. You are a dream, Penelope, my dream come true."

Tears stung in her eyes. She gave a sniff, overwhelmed. Never in her life had she heard such wonderful words--and they were about her. They meant *everything*.

"I love you." His voice gentled, becoming intimate, and he felt as if their hearts beat as one. "I know that as much as I love you now, right here today, I will love you more tomorrow and even more the day after that. And that's how it will go every day for the rest of my life."

"Oh, Nathaniel," she choked out, tears and all. This was too incredible. This was her dream come true. To be loved by a good man who loved her for her.

Nathaniel was one big blurry blob as he leaned in, pulling her against his chest. This time his kiss was lengthy, full of sweet, sweet tenderness. She was sure she felt his love in that kiss. She was sure she felt forever. She laced her fingers through his, holding on to him. This cherished moment, the most loving she'd ever known, she would treasure always. When he broke the kiss, it felt as if he was somehow still in her heart.

"This is the happiest day of my life, no question about it." He smiled down at her, his eyes bright and glinting. "I can't wait until morning to tell Evie we are going to be a family, the three of us."

"A family." Oh, how her heart rejoiced. Her own family to love. Tears burned as they spilled over her lashes. There were no words. Not a single one that could describe the rapture she felt. "We'll give her a happy life, won't we? After all she's been through, I want you to know I'm committed to that."

"I had no doubt. It's one reason why I love you so much." He raised her hand to his lips and kissed her knuckles. "This will make every difference when I talk to Quentin tomorrow. I was worried, you know, because it's nearly impossible for a bachelor to get custody of a minor girl child."

"Is it?" Penelope arched a brow and tilted her head to one side, trying to make sense of what he was saying. It was sort of hard, with joy making everything else foggy. She blinked. "What do you mean?"

"Things are pretty conservative out here in the West," he explained easily. "Bachelors aren't often given custody of a child, especially a female child. Merl is married, and the court would favor a married couple over me, regardless of how they've treated her. It's just the way things are."

"But surely because her other uncle abandoned her here--" Penelope started, wanting to argue, wanting to raise a defense and not really knowing why. Her chest was cracking. Her heart was breaking. This wasn't why Nathaniel had proposed to her, was it?

"Abandonment is serious, but it might not be enough. That's why I am determined to fight hard for her. I don't want to fail her." His voice cracked, full of a loving uncle's caring--full of love for Evie. "I won't let her go back to that, and now, because of you, she won't have to."

"Because you won't be a bachelor for long." Cold spread through her veins, slowly icing her blood. Her hands began to shake. "So, you would want to get married right away?"

"We'd have to, for Evie's sake." Nathaniel seemed pleased with himself, as kind and good as ever, but he was killing her softly.

Penelope blinked hard, trying to hold back her tears. "Evie is very, very important to you. I can see how much you love her."

Love was always a good thing. Always. Her ribs ached, drawing tight until every rib throbbed with pain. She lifted her chin, trying to be strong. "You would do anything for her."

"Absolutely. That's what you do when you love someone." He squared his shoulders, resolute, such a good uncle. Such a good man.

"Yes, that is what you do," she agreed. She untwined her fingers from his, slipping her hands away from his touch, his warmth. "I can't fault you for wanting to do anything to save her, but she's the reason you proposed to me, isn't she?"

"What?" Nathaniel quirked his brows, wrinkled his forehead, seeming truly confused.

Of course he had no clue how important this was to her. She loved him. She wanted to marry him. But she would never again make the mistake of getting engaged to a man who didn't love her. Not really. He needed her as his wife so he could keep Evie. That wasn't so different from what happened with Alexander.

She'd made the same mistake again. Every surface of her heart began to crack. Every crack began to bleed. She stood and smoothed her skirts, grappling to keep hold of her dignity. How could she have been so wrong? "I'll have a letter ready for the judge in the morning. I'll tack it on the outside of the schoolhouse door after class starts, and you can pick it up anytime. But I'm not going to marry you."

"What? But you just said--?" He stood up too, truly confused, pain etching across his handsome features. He thumbed his spectacles higher on his nose. "I don't understand, Penelope."

"You love Evie so much, and I adore you for that. That's the way it should be." She hated the sound of tears in her voice. She cleared her throat, but it didn't help. "I cannot marry someone who tells me he loves me one moment and then admits how convenient I am for him the next. That's not love. It's not what I'm looking for. I'd rather be a spinster the rest of my life than to be tied forever to a man who only sees me as useful."

"Oh, Penelope." Nathaniel's face crumpled. "I--"

But she couldn't bear to hear his explanation. He was a good man and that hurt even worse. Alexander had been a scoundrel down deep, seeking to take advantage of her tender heart for his own monetary gain. But Nathaniel, he was using her out of love for Evie. He was good down deep, very good. He just didn't truly love *her*.

She was crushed and desperate to hide it. She ran toward the entry hall. She grabbed her coat, rushing to keep ahead of his footsteps rushing after her, pounding on the floor. She launched outside, slammed the door and bolted down the steps in the brutal evening's cold, only to run into Mrs. Crabtree standing in the street.

"Ha! I knew I would catch you." Maude lifted her pointy chin, shaking a finger back and forth. "I saw you kissing that lawyer through the window. *Kissing!*"

"Excuse me, Ma'am." She rushed by the woman, stumbling in the snow, sticking her arm into her coat sleeve just as the door opened behind her. She glanced over her shoulder. Nathaniel stood in the doorway, tall and strong and limned by lamplight. She could not bear the hurt on his face, so she kept running down the street until the dark night stole her from his sight.

CHAPTER SIXTEEN

Early morning snow fell from a steel-gray clouds, swirling and dancing in mid-air. Penelope hiked her book bag higher on her shoulder, hid a yawn behind her glove and blinked snowflakes off her lashes. Usually she liked to tip her head back and watch their dizzying, delicate ballet, but not today. Her heart was too heavy. Her spirit too sad. She loved Nathaniel and that had not changed, but things between them had. They would never be the same again.

She'd trusted him to love her, and he'd let her down. Why hadn't she seen it coming? She thought it had been so amazing between them. The most incredible thing she'd ever known. She'd come to feel as if she'd always known him, as if he'd always been a part of her. How could she have been so wrong about him?

Or maybe, she'd seen what she wanted to see because she'd wanted it so very much. Just like with Alexander. Head down, she drew her scarf a little higher over her throat and crossed the snowy street. After a nearly sleepless night, she was practically asleep on her feet. She fought another yawn.

The *clip-clop* of an approaching horse broke the stillness. She snapped to attention, rubbing snow off her face. What if it was Nathaniel? Her heart jumped, beating very fast and then very slow. She didn't want to talk to him. She wasn't ready.

"Penelope!" a familiar, genteel voice called out. "Is that you, dear?"

"Aumaleigh." Delighted to see her friends' aunt, she rushed over to the approaching horse and sleigh. "What are you doing out so early? It can't be an emergency supply run for the bakery, can it?"

"Not this time." Aumaleigh laughed gently, slowing her sweet old mare to a stop. She was beauty personified with her heart-shaped face, her sleek molasses-dark curls peeking out from her knit hat, and her loving smile. "I heard about Nathaniel's custody trouble and wrote a letter of reference for him. I just wanted to catch him before he left for Deer Springs."

"How did you know?" Penelope was perpetually surprised by how fast news traveled in this tiny town. What were folks saying about her and Nathaniel?

"I am good friends with most of the gossipers," Aumaleigh answered breezily. "I also heard about your trouble with Mrs. Crabtree. She's been talking to other parents in this town, Daisy being one of them."

"Oh." Penelope thought of little Hailie and how she had blossomed with her new stepmother's love. "I am sorry if there's been any misconduct. It wasn't intentional. Perhaps I should have kept a better eye on the time."

"Love doesn't keep time," Aumaleigh said kindly. "I have written a letter on your behalf, too. I'm sure Nathaniel will make sure the superintendent sees it."

"That's very nice of you, Aumaleigh." She was touched. She swallowed hard, not knowing what else to say. The kindness of the people in this town often overwhelmed her.

"My pleasure, dear. You have a good day. I'm so happy to hear about you and Nathaniel getting along the way you are. I'm just giddy." Aumaleigh waved goodbye and reined her horse along. Apparently she hadn't heard the latest--not that anyone would know it. Nathaniel was no longer courting her. She had put an end to that.

Miserable, she trudged along, relaxing when the bell tower of the schoolhouse came into sight. Relieved to be where she belonged, she unlocked the door, stomped the snow off her shoes and shook it off her coat. Teeth chattering, she rushed to light a lamp and then the pot-bellied stove in the center of the room. Her movements echoed around her--the rasp of the match, the flare of the flame, the clink of the stove's damper as she opened it wide. All sounds that had become a wonderful part of her life, but this morning they echoed around her with a sorrowful loneliness. Nothing felt right any more. Not one thing.

In the shivering cold, Penelope sat down at her desk and held her ink bottle between her hands to warm it. Then she pulled out a sheet of parchment, dipped her quill into the ink and began to write.

She truly hoped Nathaniel was able to keep Evie. The child deserved a safe home and an uncle who loved her so much, he wanted to give her all the stability he could. But if he wanted to marry someone because it would make the difference for him gaining custody, then he would have to marry someone else. Not that she didn't want to help Evie--no, that wasn't it at all. She would have loved being Evie's aunt. Nothing would have been more wonderful. But when you wanted true love, when it was what you felt in your heart for a man, nothing less than his true love in return could be right. Otherwise, she was settling for a hollow life, a shell of what should be.

No happiness could come from that for any of them, not in the long term. She signed her name at the bottom of her letter, set her quill aside and rubbed away her tears before one of them fell on the parchment. No one could ever know about the depth of her broken heart--especially not the man responsible for the breaking.

* * *

She'd said no to him. Nathaniel piled the breakfast dishes onto the counter, feeling numb inside. He'd been that way ever since Penelope had rushed out of his house, desperate to get away from him. Those tears bright in her eyes slayed him. Like with any great wound, he couldn't feel her pain from his broken heart, but any time now the numbness was going to wear off, the shock would fade and he would be left feeling every battered piece.

She'd said no to him, and it was all his fault. That was the worst part. He shook his head, lifted his coffee cup and took one final sip before turning out the lamp. He'd finally risked opening up, she'd made it so easy that the feelings had poured out of him. But he'd ruined it all. She thought he was using her. She hadn't even let him explain.

A shadow waited by the front door. He came to a stop in the entry hall. Evie had already buttoned herself into her old coat, wearing her dilapidated shoes and sad little dress with the fraying hem. It was so short he could see her ragged stockings above her shoes. She stared at the floorboards as he shrugged into his coat.

They had a long ride ahead and it would be tough in this cold. He grabbed the bag of heating irons he'd prepared and left by the door. "Are you ready?"

Evie didn't answer. When he turned the knob, she slipped outside. She took small steps in the snow as she trailed him around the house to the stable in back. He hefted open the door and checked his pocket for Aumaleigh's letter. His chest twisted tight, grateful for the woman's kindness. Maybe her recommendation would help.

He quickly settled Evie in the sleigh with the heating irons at her feet, bundled her up well in the flannel and fur driving robes and hitched up his bay gelding. Hugh didn't look too pleased to be leaving his toasty stall, but he obediently headed out into the cold, pulling them down the eerily empty street.

Tucked on the seat next to Evie, he knew he should be thinking ahead and planning his argument to the judge. She deserved his best effort, but he couldn't concentrate. He'd been up most of the night, laying there staring at the ceiling, going over and over in his head that moment when Penelope had said no.

Her words from last night came back to him. *She's the reason you proposed to me, isn't she? I'd rather be a spinster the rest of my life than to be tied forever to a man who only sees me as useful.* He winced, closed his eyes, knowing exactly how much he'd hurt her. She'd told him about her fiancé who'd fooled her by pretending to love her for personal gain. Pain and disappointment in himself tore him apart. How could she think that of him? He opened his eyes and stared at the road without seeing it.

Well, maybe it was his fault. He'd done the one thing he'd feared. He'd failed her. Thinking back, he thought of all the ways he could have done things better between them--treated her better, done more for her, told her how he felt. Disappointed in himself, he shook his head, pain and anger tearing through him. Last night, he'd been so carried away with the power of his love for her that he'd rushed things. Now he'd lost her.

The horse came to a stop and he realized he'd pulled back on the reins. The schoolhouse loomed over them, cozy with lamplight shining golden in the windows and gray smoke curling out of the stovepipe. He swiped snow off his face, climbed out of the sleigh and headed toward the single piece of parchment tucked into the door, faintly flapping in the wind.

His chest coiled up into one excruciating knot. It took a Herculean effort to lift his foot and place it on the bottom step. It felt as if that letter was a final goodbye, the last piece of closeness he would have to Penelope. He needed that letter, but he didn't want to take it. Snow blew in beneath the brim of his hat, striking his face. When he looked up, he caught sight of her through the window.

She stood at the front of the class, slender and willowy, lovely as always. Her hair was up in a soft knot, and wisps of light curls tumbled down to caress the sides of her face. The white shirtwaist she wore brought out the luster of her complexion. She was holding a book open, speaking to three students who stood before her. Her gaze slipped past them and arrowed straight to him, as if she felt his presence.

The pain in his chest stilled. He felt a connection to her when their gazes held. He saw her pain and her distrust in him. He could see the wound in her heart. He knew without words that he'd broken her trust. Once that was gone, he had no way to repair it. No way to redeem himself. She closed her heart to him, ripped her gaze away and focused on her students. But even from a distance, he could see the shine of tears in her eyes.

His eyes stung too. Hands shaking, he grabbed the letter, pulling it out between the frame and the door. He hadn't intended to read it, he didn't think he could stand to, but the wind snatched the corner, flipping the bottom third of the page open and he caught her beautifully written words.

While Mr. Nathaniel Denby is a bachelor and I understand it is highly unusual to trust a bachelor with the care of a minor female child, I know Mr. Denby personally and have watched him take excellent care of little Evie. She arrived in my classroom silent, withdrawn and I fear abused, unable to even speak. While living with Mr. Denby, she has begun to grow into a happy child. She has made friends, has become more out-going and has started to have hope for her life. As her teacher, I believe placing her anywhere else would be detrimental to her well-being. Mr. Denby has shown great commitment to his niece, doing anything it takes to ensure her safety and happiness. Any child would be lucky to be in his care. Please give Evie the chance at happiness she deserves and let her stay with Nathaniel.

Sincerely,
Penelope Shalvis

His vision blurred, so he stopped reading. He tucked the letter into his coat pocket next to Aumaleigh's, moved beyond reason by those kind words--even when he didn't deserve them from her.

And that's exactly why he loved Penelope so much.

The wind gusted, as if eager to push him away from her. He didn't remember climbing down the steps or crossing the schoolyard. He stumbled getting into the sleigh and dropped the reins twice when he reached for them. He was a mess, no doubt about it. Losing Penelope was the most painful thing he'd ever done.

He blinked, pulling out his watch to check the time. He wanted to get to court early to make sure the judge had room on his docket for them. He shook the reins, Hugh lunged forward and pulled them down the road. He cut a sideways glance at his niece. She hadn't moved from the last time he'd checked on her, still with her head down, staring straight ahead, as motionless as a doll.

That's when he spotted Nelson Eddles, the superintendent, turning onto the street behind them. The man pulled his horse to a stop in front of the schoolhouse, looking grim. Looking like he meant business.

A bad feeling settled in Nathaniel's gut. He remembered spotting Mrs. Crabtree on the street last night when Penelope fled, and realization hit him like a falling brick. The superintendent wasn't paying a social call. He'd come to fire Penelope.

And it was his fault.

CHAPTER SEVENTEEN

The image of Nathaniel standing in the snow holding onto her letter haunted her all morning. It stayed in her mind, refusing to budge as she quizzed her eighth grade geography students, read arithmetic problems to her fourth graders and listened to her adorable seven-year-olds attempt to spell.

"Uh--?" Sally Gray wrinkled her forehead, staring at the ceiling. "W-- A-- K?"

Sally arched her eyebrow at the end, perhaps hoping her cuteness would make up for the fact she hadn't studied.

"No." Penelope did her best to keep a straight but slightly stern face. "That was almost right, but not quite. Hailie, can you spell 'walk'?"

"But Miss Shalvis, it's lunch time." Hailie Kincaid, Daisy's sweet stepdaughter, clasped her hands together like an angel. "I can spell 'lunch'."

"That won't be necessary." She closed the speller, setting the book on the corner of her desk. "You two girls will be taking this lesson over. I'm afraid Sally is proving to be a bad influence on you, Hailie. Ilsa, you may study the next list of words in your book. You three may return to your seats."

The three little girls whipped around to rush back to their desks, Ilsa trailing, her red braids bobbing. Every eye in the schoolroom turned toward the front, watching Penelope's every move while she shelved the elementary speller. Anticipation popped in the air, as students leaned forward in their desks waiting for her to say the words. "It's lunchtime. You are dismissed."

Boys shot out of their chairs. Girls started talking. The pleasant sound of happy children rang in the air, although it was suddenly a very chilly air. Penelope shivered, turning toward the gust coming from the newly opened door.

Footsteps knelled in the vestibule, coming closer, heavy and solemn. Alarm fluttered in her chest, as if she knew what was coming. The kids in the room fell silent as a tall, somber man in his sixties entered the classroom. She recognized him right away. Nelson Eddles, the superintendent, swept off his hat.

"Miss Shalvis." He looked as grim as a judge at a funeral.

"I'm afraid we need to talk."

Her heart stopped. It just stalled dead in her chest, refusing to beat. Mrs. Crabtree's threat leaped into mind. There was no excuse for last night, for her violating her morality clause. It had been the last thing on her mind, what with her heart broken. She swallowed hard and pulled over a wooden chair from the corner for the man to sit in.

"Please sit down," she invited, fighting to keep her voice from shaking. "Would you like a cup of hot tea?"

"I'm in no mood for tea, I'm afraid." Mr. Eddles folded his big frame into the chair, turning his back to the classroom. "Late yesterday evening, Mrs. Crabtree knocked at my door, concerned over the kind of woman teaching her children."

"Yes, I am aware of Mrs. Crabtree's claim." Miserable, Penelope sank into her chair. She folded her hands on her desk, bracing herself. This was not going to go well. Thankfully, most of the children were leaving for a warm meal at home. As if sensing the seriousness of the visit, the remaining children filed out into the vestibule and closed the door behind them. Which meant none of her beloved students would see what would happen next.

"You are aware of the morality clause in your contract, Miss Shalvis." Mr. Eddles cleared his throat.

"Yes." She sat up straighter, squared her shoulders and looked the man in the eyes. Embarrassment filled her. "You explained it to me when I came to sign the contract back in September."

"Yes, and I told you how important it was to abide by it." The superintendent winced, obviously sorry. "Mrs. Crabtree spoke of three incidents. There was a public kiss and twice you were alone and unchaperoned with a man past seven o'clock in the evening. I believe the third incident included a kiss also."

"It's all true. I'm sorry." She had no excuse. She stared down at the ink blotter on her desk, feeling her stomach fall. He was going to fire her. He had every right to. It was his job to. She lifted her chin, ready to accept her fate. "It's my fault. I did violate the clause. It wasn't intentional, but nothing improper happened. You have my word of honor."

"I believe you, Miss Shalvis, but that doesn't change the facts of your behavior." He arched a dark, bushy brow. "When I left my house this morning, I came here to fire you."

His words echoed in the empty classroom. She hung her head. Tears scorched her eyes and she willed them away. "Thank you for being so kind about it, Mr. Eddles. You have to know this is breaking my heart."

"You've been a fine teacher, Miss Shalvis. Believe me, coming here to fire you wasn't what I wanted to do." Mr. Eddles rose out of his chair. "So I was very glad when Nathaniel Denby stopped me in the street this morning and spoke to me. He took entire responsibility for the incidents. He explained about his niece's injured hand and then how he'd proposed to you last night."

"That was nice of him to try and help." It was just like him to intervene. She rose on trembling knees and splayed her hand on the desktop to steady herself. "I want to make this easy on you, Mr. Eddles. I've loved this job so much--"

Her throat closed, so she couldn't continue. She took a moment, trying to relax, trying to control her emotions. This was a hard let down, a bitter disappointment, but she had no one to be upset with but herself. It felt as if the earth had opened up beneath her feet and she was falling. She thought of her father's predictions that she couldn't make it out here on her own, and then she shook her head. No, she'd done just fine. She'd built an amazing life here in Bluebell, Montana Territory. She'd come into her own, and she was stronger than she'd ever thought. Without a doubt, she could get through this too.

"I'll clean out my desk right away." She bobbed her head, determined and grateful. "And again, Mr. Eddles, I am sorry. My time here has been some of my best. Thank you for the opportunity to have taught at your school."

"Well, it's been my pleasure to have you. And by the way, I don't want you to clear out your desk." Mr. Eddles took a backwards step. His frown became less severe. "Nathaniel spent a good part of the morning arguing with me and the school board until they agreed to put you on probation. As long as you make no more violations and write an apology to the board, we would like to keep you on until the end of the school year."

"What? You're not firing me?" Her jaw fell open. Had she heard him right? "Mr. Eddles, are you really going to let me keep teaching?"

"Yes. Now, I don't want to be the one to stand in the way of romance. Say yes to the poor man." The somber man winked, donned his hat and strode from the room, leaving her speechless. Fresh pain rolled into her heart.

Nathaniel had done this. He'd done it for her. Longing battered her. She missed him. She missed seeing his smile and the warmth in his eyes when he looked at her. She longed for the sweetness of being with him, trying to salvage a burned meal in the kitchen or sliding with him down a steep snowdrift. She eased down into her chair before her knees gave out entirely. She wished his love had been real, what she'd wanted it so desperately to be.

Now that the superintendent had gone, the remaining students wandered back in to eat their lunches by the stove. She smiled reassuringly at them, relieved that at least she had her job. She might be unlucky in love, but she had her teaching. And that was mighty fine.

"Evie!" Sadie Gray abandoned her lunch and dashed across the room, her shoes drumming on the floorboards. "You came! If you hurry and eat your lunch fast with me, we can go out and play dodgeball with snowballs."

Evie? Surprised, Penelope looked up, had to blink twice to make sure the girl was really there. Wearing her worn-thin, ill-fitting, patched dress, Evie padded into the classroom in her quiet way.

They hadn't gone to see the judge. The realization hit her like a speeding train. Penelope pushed to her feet. Something the superintendent said rushed back to her now, and she realized the meaning of it. *Nathaniel spent a good part of the morning arguing with the school board.* Which meant Nathaniel hadn't been able to get to the courthouse in time to be placed on the day's docket. He'd missed his chance with the judge.

That he'd done for her, too. Tears filled her eyes. Every kindness he'd ever shown her, every good deed he'd ever done for her and all his sweet tenderness came rushing back to her. She had to at least thank him for what he'd done, and she needed to do it now. She glanced around the room at the remaining students. Eloise Crabtree sat in the back row, at her desk, reading from a book Penelope had lent her. Perfect. Penelope grabbed her shawl off the back of her chair.

"Eloise. You're in charge." She swept the shawl over her shoulders, making a beeline toward the door. "I'll be back in a few minutes."

She felt the students staring at her curiously, but that didn't stop her. She was rushing, jogging, then running through the vestibule and down the stairs toward the lone man in a horse-drawn sleigh driving away from the school--driving away from her. Sweet agony filled her as she savored the familiar sight of him--the tilt of his Stetson, the square, steady strength in his shoulders, the ruffle of his dark hair against his collar, blown by the wind. She still loved him. She feared she always would.

"Penelope." Nathaniel's baritone rumbled coolly, carried by the wind. He'd turned around his horse and sleigh and was coming toward her, so close she could hear the chilly tone in his voice.

Not that she blamed him. She did turn down his proposal.

"Mr. Eddles was just here," she called out. "He told me what you did."

"I was only doing the right thing." He stopped his sleigh, looking right past her at the schoolhouse behind her.

Looking at him hurt her. It made every jagged, broken shard of her heart bleed all over again. He'd only been trying to save Evie. She'd been the one dreaming of romance. But it had felt so real. Every look, every touch, every kiss.

"I always do the right thing." He drew his horse to a stop, climbed from the sleigh and headed straight toward her. "Always. No matter what. I choose the right thing every single time. I thought you knew me well enough to understand that."

"I thought I did, too." She held up one hand, hoping to stop his approach. He was too close. She could see the smooth shaven angle of his jaw and the hurt in his indigo blue eyes. She remembered the bliss of being held in his arms, tight against his chest. Memories welled up, bringing with them all the affection she had for him. Every single bit. "You were trying to do the right thing for Evie."

"No, I was trying to do the right thing for you." He came to a stop in front of her, towering over her, mighty and true, looking like every hero she'd ever read about, every dream she'd ever had. Snow crested his hat and caught in his dark hair as he leaned in closer. "That's what today was all about."

"I know that. And I appreciate that more than you know." Snow brushed against her cheek, and she swiped it away. "You know how important my job is to me."

"I do. I wouldn't want you to lose it over me." He reached in to help her brush off some of the snow catching in the soft curls around her face. "I should have been more careful of your morals clause and none of this would have happened."

"I bear the responsibility, it's my contract," she said, disappointment darkening her hazel eyes. She looked down at the ground between them, perhaps to hide her reaction.

She'd misunderstood him. Well, he'd better try this again.

"I am the man," he informed her, moving in to take her hand. Surprise lit her face when his fingers closed around hers. His heart squeezed. Nothing had ever felt as right as this moment. He gentled his voice. "I take care of you, that's the way it is, because I love you. In fact, I love you so much, you overwhelm me."

"Wait. You do? I mean, I do?" She arched a slender brow, her face adorably puzzled. She had no clue. Not a single one.

And that was his fault, too. He'd fallen miserably short in opening up to her. Words failed him when it came to his feelings, but he would get better at it starting here, starting now. He set his shoulders, determined to be the man she needed.

"You leave me in a muddle," he confessed. "Last night when we were talking, my heart had never felt so full. I have never felt so much. I have no experience with this kind of all-encompassing love. And it's because of you, Penelope."

"Me?" She gazed up at him, not quite willing to believe.

"You befuddle me and overwhelm me." He bared his soul. "I got carried away on the rush of my feelings. They were so strong, they overpowered logic, and I should have slowed down. I should have made sure you knew all along exactly how I felt. So when I proposed to you and jumped right into talking marriage, you didn't think for even one split second that my feelings were genuine. I'm sorry for breaking your heart. I promise if you give me a second chance I will not fail you again."

Her lower lip trembled. Now it was her turn to be overwhelmed. She couldn't speak. Staring up into his face, etched with sincerity, into his eyes that showed how afraid he was to lose her, she saw the same heartbreak she'd felt. Not until this moment did she realize the problem. She didn't truly believe she would ever be loved completely. That she could be endlessly treasured and truly happy for the rest of her life. But that's what she read in his eyes. She felt it in his heart.

When she splayed her hand on his chest, she felt the steady beat of his heart. Her world changed. Realization passed through her like a satisfied sigh. This was her chance. This was her fairytale love and she was not going to let it pass her by. She'd found a wonderful man, true of heart, a man who she could trust to always do the right thing, to always do right by her. She could see that now. She wasn't going to let anything stop her. Not her fear, not her self-doubts, not one thing. She was going to believe.

"I have one question." She curled her fingers into the fabric of his coat. "Is it too late to change my answer to your proposal?"

"It's never too late, not for you." Fear vanished from his eyes. Relief passed across his handsome, dear face. "I would wait forever for you. You are the only one for me, Penelope. You are my one and only for the rest of my life. I love you, how I love you."

No truer words had ever been spoken. Tears filled Penelope's eyes. Love filled her heart. Perfect, blissful, endless love. He cradled her face in his hands, tender, as if she were the most precious treasure he would ever hold. Yes, she thought, her eyes blurring. He was her dream. He was her everything. She leaned her forehead against his, gazing into his eyes. The world vanished until there was only the two of them--one man and one woman desperately in love.

The sun chose that moment to shine through the falling snow, haloing them with a golden glow. It was a sign, and they both knew it. Penelope smiled. Their life together was going to be better than any book she'd ever read, far better than any dream. She just knew it.

EPILOGUE

Saturday afternoon

Gabriel took one last look around the cozy log kitchen house on the Rocking M Ranch and tried to hold his heart still. Very still. Aumaleigh wasn't here, that was the only saving grace and the only reason he agreed to drop by his sister's place of employment on his way out of town. It wasn't easy leaving. It wasn't easy seeing the place where Aumaleigh had lived, worked and now owned. He tried not to think of her as he gave his sister a final hug.

"I'll write you as soon as we reach home," he promised, taking a step back in the warm but empty kitchen. All the other employees were up at the main house apparently making last minute preparations for a wedding. One of Aumaleigh's nieces was tying the knot. He knew because he'd heard about it around town. In a place as small as Bluebell, weddings were big news.

"You'd better write me and write often." Josslyn blinked tears from her eyes. She pretended to be too tough to cry. "Now that we've put our differences to rest, we should keep in touch. Neither one of us is getting any younger."

"That's the truth." He studied his sister. She was tough, honest and kind. He wished life had been easier on her. He wished he had been, too. When Aumaleigh had broken his heart, she'd broken him. He'd never been the same man. Not ever again. As much as he regretted that, he accepted that the past was over. Now--today--was what mattered.

"Maybe you'll invite me to Seth's wedding?"

"There's no wedding yet. Don't jump the gun." Josslyn shook her head at him, as if disapproving, but he spotted the spark of excitement in her eyes.

"A wedding is inevitable." That was the plain truth. He backed toward the door, buttoning his coat all the way. That boy was in love with pretty Rose McPhee. Those two belonged together. "Besides, I'd like to come back and see you again."

"Any time." Now tears pooled in her eyes, and she couldn't blink fast enough to keep up with them. "I suppose I might be able to tolerate you again."

"I suppose I could tolerate it, too." He unhooked his Stetson from the wall peg and spotted a shawl hanging there on the low row of otherwise empty pegs. His chest squeezed tight as a fist. That was Aumaleigh's shawl. He knew without asking. He'd recognize her delicate, precise knitting anywhere.

It was odd how well you could come to know another person. Even after all this time and all the life that had happened along the way, he could recall her sitting on the porch on a summer's evening or by the hearth in the winter knitting away, her steel needles clacking a merry rhythm. Loss hit him so hard it nearly brought him to his knees. Sorrow dug deep as he plopped his hat on his head and reached for the doorknob. That place in his heart was always going to hold love for her. It looked as if he would have to learn to accept that. All the anger in the world could not dim it or put it out.

He stepped into the soft winter sunshine, let the cool wind blow over him as he looked at his sister one last time. Time has carried them down different paths, but he was glad their paths had intersected again.

With a few last words to Josslyn, he strode out into the sunshine where his team waited. He could see the faint outline of a rooftop through the trees far up the hill. Plumes of gray smoke curled, rising from several chimneys. That's where Aumaleigh was, he thought, ignoring the pang in his heart. This was goodbye. She'd treated him badly. She'd taken his naive heart and crushed it callously, but he wished her well. He wished her the best.

* * *

"Penelope!" Rose threw open McPhee Manor's front door, looking adorable in pale pink chiffon. Her blond curls tumbled down to brush her oval face, highlighting her big blue eyes and ear-to-ear grin. "It's good to see you. I'm glad you could come."

"Where else would I be? I wouldn't miss Annie's wedding. Not for the world." She strode in, carrying her gaily wrapped gift and spotted a table in the entryway already sporting several wedding presents. She added hers to the pile before tugging off her gloves. "How are things going? Do you need any last minute help? I came a little early just in case. When you're preparing for a wedding, nothing ever goes as planned."

"You've got that right." Rose took the scarf and hung it up. "But thankfully it's just close friends and family. It's easier to manage. Iris and I finished the cake this morning. Most of Aumaleigh's cooks are in the kitchen madly slicing and chopping."

"Wonderful." Penelope unbuttoned her coat. She was glad to be here among friends, full of joy for this happy occasion.

"Is that Penelope?" Magnolia's voice drifted down from above where she peeked around the corner of the nearby staircase. She was lovely in light blue chiffon. "Ooh, it's good to see you. I'm waiting for the next installment of your and Nathaniel's love story."

"So am I," Rose chimed in. "But I wanted to wait a few minutes before I just jumped in and asked. I have manners, Magnolia."

"I have them, too." Magnolia gave a light laugh, disappearing down the upstairs hall. "I seem to have misplaced mine, though. Tell me if you find them."

"She thinks she's funny," Rose explained, taking Penelope's coat and hanging it up for her. "But I really am dying of curiosity. Everyone was talking about your tender moment in front of the school, with Nathaniel's forehead to yours, gazing into each other's eyes with great love. You know, after he saved your job."

"Yes, I want to hear all about it." Daisy paraded into sight, looking lovely in a lavender dress skimming her slender curves. She was radiant. "Tell us what happened next."

"Well, I invited him and Evie over for supper last night." She sighed. She couldn't help it. All it took was one thought of Nathaniel--instant happiness. "We had a lovely time. Evie seems very happy that her uncle is courting me. Daisy, we may have something in common very soon."

"We both might have instant but wonderful daughters." Daisy took Penelope by the hand and gave her a squeeze. "It's a special thing Hailie and I share. I can't take her mother's place, and I would never want to, but every time she calls me Ma, my heart brims over. She is my joy."

"Penelope!" Verbena bounded out of the kitchen. Stunning in sage green, she rushed down the hallway. "Annie was just asking about you. She's a nervous wreck wearing Aumaleigh's dress, but we said she can change out of it before we eat. She's afraid of spilling something on it."

"I can't imagine how lovely she must look." Penelope sighed, remembering the exquisite lace and pearl dress each McPhee girl had worn at their weddings. First Verbena, then Daisy and now Annie. It was a tradition of love, the very best kind.

"Come into the library." Rose invited, leading the way. "Poor Oscar spent the last two days getting it ready for us."

"And we kept changing our minds, making him move things back and forth." Magnolia shook her head as she reappeared on the staircase, hurrying toward them. "Poor Oscar. I am going to bake him a cake. It's the least he deserves."

"You mean I'll be the one baking the cake," Iris corrected ruefully from the far end of the library where dozens of little candles burned like fairy lights. The sofas had been realigned to face the big bay window, where sunlight tumbled through the panes like grace, like hope. Soft panels of chiffon and lace intertwined over a white archway, where the couple would stand for their vows.

"It's beautiful. It's breathtaking." Penelope took in every detail, every bit of love and care the sisters had put into this wedding for their cousin.

"Annie wanted something small and modest, so this is what we came up with," Rose explained. Her mouth was open to say more, but a knock sounded upon the door. "I'll get that. I know Oscar is busy somewhere. Take a seat, Penelope and get comfortable. That's probably the minister now. We're almost ready to start!"

Penelope didn't get the chance to sit down. Their friends Elise and Gemma had arrived, and right behind them was the minister and then the handsome groom. Shy Adam looked uncomfortable with all the attention as he entered the library, but what a striking groom he made in his black suit.

Beckett arrived with Hailie. Zane came in with several of the cowboys from the ranch, Gil included. Maebry breezed in, sipping ginger water to keep her morning sickness at bay. Tyler strolled in to take Magnolia by the hand. Seth arrived, stealing Rose away to presumably steal a private kiss.

The final knock on the door was Nathaniel's. How good he looked in his suit, with Evie at his side. He would be leaving on Monday to make the long trek to track down the traveling judge. Penelope had a feeling it would turn out well for them. Evie rushed up to say hello, but Hailie and Bea politely invited her to the kitchen for a cookie and they disappeared.

"You've never looked more beautiful." Nathaniel took her by the hand, pulling her to a quiet corner of the room. "I still can't believe you're really mine. I'm the luckiest guy in the room."

"And I'm the luckiest girl." She laced her fingers between his. The warmth of his touch zinged through her, soul deep. "The next wedding in town is going to be ours."

"Yes it is." Joy lit up his indigo blue eyes, but it was the love that shone there that mattered the most. He leaned closer to press his forehead to hers. Gazing into her eyes like this, it was as if they were one. A smile tugged at the corners of his mouth. "To think we've managed to keep that piece of news to ourselves. No one knows our big day is tomorrow."

"That is truly an accomplishment in this nosy town," she teased. "Besides, we don't want to upstage Annie and Adam's wedding. This is their day."

"And our day is coming." Bliss rumbled in his deep voice and he leaned in, slanting his mouth over hers.

It was a perfect kiss. Flawless and tender in every possible way. Just like their love was and would always be. A love like this came around once in a woman's life, and if she were lucky--very, very lucky--it would last the rest of her life. Gazing into Nathaniel's eyes with his kiss tingling on her lips, she knew their future was going to be sweet. The sweetest one of all.

"It's time!" Magnolia shouted above the din of conversation in the room. Folks milled into place, conversation turned to whispers and then to silence as Aumaleigh walked into the library. She was stunning in light yellow, proudly walking the lovely young bride down the aisle.

Annie looked incandescent with joy and hope, and when she looked down the aisle at the man waiting for her, tears slipped down her cheeks. There was nothing more precious than true love.

The whole room sighed at the sweet sight of Annie and Adam exchanging solemn and loving vows. It was one more happily-ever-after for the McPhee family. And as Penelope gazed around the room at Iris and Aumaleigh, she had the suspicion there would be more happy endings to come--and she just couldn't wait.

The McPhee Clan continues with Iris's story, *Dreams of You*, coming late this summer.

ABOUT THE AUTHOR

Jillian Hart makes her home in Washington State, where she has lived most of her life. When Jillian is not writing away on her next book, she can be found reading, going to lunch with friends and spending quiet evenings at home with her family.

Made in the USA
Lexington, KY
21 July 2014